Homer & Karen

LOVE IS LIKE
AN ACORN

LOVE IS LIKE AN ACORN

AN ACORN

by Matsu Crawford

Author of *For Every Red Sea* and *To Make the Wounded Whole*

ZONDERVAN PUBLISHING HOUSE

GRAND RAPIDS, MICHIGAN

LOVE IS LIKE AN ACORN

1

MINORU TADA WALKED slowly up the alley toward his home. Every step was an effort for him; his body seemed weighted with sorrow. The long walk from the cemetery made him feel suddenly old for his eighteen years.

The alley was so familiar to him, he had but to glance at the fences along the way to know whose home he was passing. The Yamada's had recently replaced their old bamboo fence with another exactly like the old one, except now the new bamboo stalks were edged with a greenish tinge. The Yoshida's fence made of woven twigs was now so old and brittle, one felt that one day they would turn to a stack of black dirt. Only the Matsuda's fence was of galvanized wire, allowing anyone to look into their neatly kept garden. This kind of fence was unknown before the war; now it was being used all over Japan by those who sought new and modern ways of doing things.

Looking at the fences as he walked along, Minoru remembered the first time he had walked with his grandfather beside the newly-strung wire fence. While he had been admiring the novel aspects of it, his grandfather, walking beside him, had struck at the wire with his walking stick; then spat contemptuously into the dirt beside it. His grandfather had not voiced his anger but Minoru had wondered about a connection between an old man's anger and a fence made of wire. Thinking of this now, Minoru realized that there were many things about the old man which had puzzled him.

At the turn of the alley his home could be seen, an old-style Japanese house with just the weather-beaten tile roof, showing patches of gray-green moss. It seemed to crouch in the thick garden shrubs which surrounded it.

The house stood on an abrupt rise of ground making a dark glob at the end of the road. At the front gate of the house one might turn to see the town of Takarazuka which followed the curve of the river, with mountains rising in the background. At night, when the lights were on, and the great theater district was aglow with the flashing neon signs, the scene was gay and intriguing.

When he was a child, before his mother tucked him between his futons for the night, she sometimes brought him to sit with her for a few minutes, before the garden gate, to watch the lights come on over the city. He remembered her saying once, not particularly to him, but to the gathering darkness about them, as she looked toward the theater district, "It's a diamond brooch at the heart of the city." Once, Minoru had added that the lights leading up the hills along the roads were "jewels on a string."

Here in this house Minoru had grown up; in it his mother had been born, and his grandfather and his father before him. It had been the home of the Takahashi family for six generations. Minoru looked at the place now as if he were seeing it for the first time. He stopped in his progress toward it to look again, realizing that he was now seeing it as his own.

Until today, it had been his grandfather's home; now it was his. It was as if he were returning from a far country and was seeing it after an absence of many days.

Three days before his grandfather sank in a coma, Minoru had gone into the room to find the old man awake, lying on his futon, weak and wasted from weeks of suffering. He had managed to roll over on his side to face his grandson and to say in a surprisingly strong voice,

"You are to carry on here, Minoru, as all who have gone before you have done. All that I have in this world is yours." He had smiled then and turned his face away.

As he remembered now the gentle look on his grandfather's always stern face, tears flooded his eyes and he stumbled on a stone lying in the way. Quickly drying his tears, he began to walk more hurriedly toward the tall wooden fence surrounding his home. He pushed the gate open just wide enough to allow him to enter, then deliberately pushed it shut behind him. He wanted nothing so much, at this moment, as to be alone.

Minoru had had enough of company during the past three days. The house and garden had been overrun with neighbors, friends and business associates of his grandfather. In a matter of hours after the tired old man had closed his eyes in death, word of it had gone through the town in which his life had been spent.

At first Minoru could not bring himself to enter the lonely house. He went to sit upon the huge rock in the garden where his grandfather rested after puttering about the garden in the late afternoons, examining each shrub and flower bed as if they awaited his inspection. Minoru looked about the spot with new appreciation of the old man's loving toil. There was a burnished look about the place; the plants and shrubs now done with blooming, were heavy and vibrant in the new glossy growth of summer, giving an extra freshness to the garden plot.

For one fleeting moment, Minoru seemed to see the old man standing beside the rock near the pool, where he so often stood at twilight, smoking his pipe in meditative silence. There in the early mornings he often came to watch his goldfish dart like streaks of gold in the morning sunlight filtering through the clear water of the pool.

Minoru shook his head as if to rid himself of this haunting vision of the one whose cremated remains he had witnessed interred in the old cemetery back of the temple that very afternoon.

He shivered in the misty veil of darkness which seemed now to be folding upon the garden. At that moment a light went on in the house, and he was reminded that Obasan (servant) would be wondering why he was so late in coming home. Somehow he had forgotten that he would not be entirely alone tonight. Obasan had been so definitely a part of the house, he had not given a thought to her or to her sorrow over the definite closing of a stage in her own life.

She had been in the house as long as Minoru could remember, performing her lowly tasks, seeming to get her greatest pleasure in serving others of the household. In this service she had become old and stooped, yet she had outlived his mother, his grandmother and now his grandfather — all of those who had made up his childhood world.

The light which Obasan had turned on seemed to put life into the dark, lonely house. It did not seem so bereft now. Minoru was thankful for Obasan — the last link with the family he had known.

As Minoru pushed back the door of the genkan, the little bronze bell tinkled almost gaily. Immediately the paper door slid back, there was Obasan on her knees on the straw mat, welcoming the new master of the house. Tonight she was making their new relationship quite plain in giving him the welcome reserved for the master of the house.

When the old woman raised her head from its contact with her hands laid flat on the floor, she leaned back on her heels to look full into Minoru's youthful, troubled face. There was love for him in her small black eyes, almost buried in multitudinous wrinkles. Minoru's heart lifted at the familiar sight of her.

So well did she know this boy, whom she had helped to bring to manhood, she refrained from all conversation. His heart was too heavy with his loss, for the grandfather was the only father the boy had ever known. She too missed the master and she knew the weight of sorrow in this young man. Rising from her squatting position, she gave an extra bow.

"Go to the cool spot on the rokka (porch), Minoru," she said softly. "I have placed a zabuton (cushion) there where you are sure to catch a breeze. There I will bring your dinner when you are ready for it."

Minoru bowed his thanks without speaking and turned up the stairs to his room. There he laid aside the hot yōfuku (foreign suit) in exchange for a cool, cotton kimona. He had left his shoes at the door; he now removed his socks and slipped his bare feet into loose straw sandals.

As he passed the kitchen door, the smell of broiled fish assailed his nostrils. This was his favorite food; Obasan had remembered. But tonight he had no appetite for anything she had prepared for him.

He paused in his progress toward the porch, to watch Obasan busily arranging the tray artistically as she was accustomed to do all the days that he had known her. Her familiar movements about the dark kitchen caused things to swing back to reality for Minoru. They were back at home again doing accustomed things, and though the others were away never to return, life would go on, and, somehow, he would adjust to it in time.

As he knelt on the soft zabuton, placed on the polished floor for him, Minoru had the impulse to go to his room for the only chair the house could boast. He checked this impulse. It was too soon to break away from the bond which his grandfather had thrown about him. There would be plenty of time for change; he would have it come gradually in keeping with his sense of filial piety.

His grandfather had allowed this one chair in his Japanese home when Minoru had made the plea: it would be advantageous for the long hours of study during high school days. Even then the old man had grumbled about the youth of the land turning too readily to foreign ways and comforts, rejecting, as inferior, the ways of Old Japan.

Waiting for his dinner to be brought to him, Minoru spent the interval remembering the night that he had first dared to broach the subject of a chair for his room. . . .

"You see, Ojiisan (grandfather), we do not sit on our legs at school anymore. All the years that I have been in school we have sat upon benches. My legs are not accustomed to floorsitting as yours are. Neither did you, as a boy, have to spend such long hours at your studies as we do." That was all that he had said; his grandfather had spoken not a word but had continued to smoke his pipe in silence. No argument ever changed the old man's mind, Minoru knew. He also knew that he could only state his case; the ultimate decision would be Ojiisan's.

Sometimes, but not often, the old man's will could be changed by common-sense reasoning, but he was almost always adamant where foreign ways were concerned, and a chair was definitely a foreign object. Not only did his grandfather reject these ways, he spurned them with a sort of hatred which had frightened Minoru in his younger days.

The next day, however, to Minoru's surprise, he had returned from school to find not only a chair but a matching desk in his room. Thus, Minoru learned early in life that his grandfather's ambition for him in the scholastic world was something to conjure with.

Obasan broke into these thoughts by slipping to her knees beside him as she placed the tray in front of him upon the floor. She did not leave him but sat waiting to see whether he would eat the things she had prepared for him. If he did not eat, Minoru knew, she would begin to coax him as she used to do when he was a small child. That he could not bear tonight. He picked up his chopsticks and lifted a piece of the fish to his mouth. Once it was in, and being masticated to her satisfaction, the old servant rose to her feet and slippered back to her kitchen.

The food tasted better than Minoru had expected. When he thought of it this was the first real meal he'd had in the past three days. He found himself eating with relish as he washed down the food with steaming tea. When Obasan came to take away the tray, she clucked with satisfaction at the sight of the empty dishes.

"It was delicious, Obasan. Thank you," he said.

"I am glad that you forced yourself to eat, Minoru. Even sorrows can be pushed aside by good food, if only one will force himself to eat."

Minoru realized that she was definitely setting a new relationship between the two of them, pushing him into the role of master of the house. He was not sure that he liked this new relationship.

"Is there anything else you would like?" she asked him in tones always reserved for the grandfather.

"Not a thing, thank you, Obasan," he told her.

Unfolding from her squatting position, at the same time lifting the tray from the floor, she returned with it to the kitchen. In a short time she was back, standing beside him, holding in her hands a canvas packet securely tied with a string.

"Your grandfather entrusted this to me days before he became nothing, with the instruction that I should place it in your hands after all was over with him." The old servant bowed lower than her usual stoop and put the packet into Minoru's hands. She turned again to her kitchen and there in the door bowed again to say, "Oyasumi na sai" (Goodnight).

"Oyasumi na sai," Minoru answered her.

Long after Minoru heard the old woman go up to her room padding softly on the back stairs, he sat still, holding the packet in his hands, staring out into the velvety blackness of the garden, absently watching the fireflies threading golden threads in and out of the bushes as if decorating for the fairies.

He remembered once, long ago, returning home with his grandfather across the back field. They had noticed a small tree aglow with the eerie light of fireflies. Minoru had suddenly squealed with delight, "Ojiisan, look! The fireflies are having a picnic." He had been filled with delight at such an unusual sight.

The old man had chuckled. "In a way they *are* having a picnic. Actually they are signalling their mates with flashlights. It is mating-time for them, and they all seem to know it." Here he had checked his speech abruptly, not wanting to open a discussion for which this child was not ready. He was still innocent of such things. After a few moments of silence still walking side by side, his grandfather had said almost harshly. "At least, even the fireflies know enough to stick to their own kind in the world of nature. Anything else is wrong, and leads to no good."

Minoru had not understood what the old man was trying to say, but he somehow had the feeling that the words were meant for him. So often during Minoru's youth, his grandfather had said puzzling things which he could not understand. Very early in life, he came to know that these cutting things had to do with him in someway. When the statements were made in the presence of his mother there were tears, and a tangible, ugly feeling came into the room.

He could remember that on such nights, his mother would draw him from his own futon over to her own, and, holding him very close to her body, wet the back of his head with her tears.

Thinking of these things now, Minoru wondered why Ojiisan had never discussed the accident of his birth with him when he grew older. He had always known that something about him was different. Even from his kindergarten days, he had felt a stigma attached to him when his little playmates had whispered, "Gaijin" (foreigner) behind his back. He often went into his mother's room to squat before her long mirror to examine his face reflected there. He looked like no foreigner, neither did he look like his Japanese playmates. His skin was whiter and there was a rosy glow beneath it. His eyes were brown, not beady black like his playmates', and they were round shaped, wide open. His hair was not jet black and there was a tendency for it to bunch up over his brow. His mother had kept it cropped close to his head so that the curl would not show. Now that Minoru was a man, he wore it longer, so the wave would show. He liked it.

In his early boyhood, Minoru became accustomed to being stared at when he went out into the street. Often, at home when they sat about the table, he would catch his grandfather studying him closely through eyes that were almost black slits. It had made him uncomfortable and shy.

Once when they thought he was in the garden playing he had heard his grandfather and grandmother in their room having words about him.

"You blame the child for something for which he is *not* to blame. It was none of his doings," he had heard his grandmother say hotly.

"It is not that I blame the child, I am simply ashamed to walk abroad with a half-blood child. I can never forget that he is different, and it hurts. Never was there such a disgrace in the Takahashi family."

"The child is a person," he had heard his grandmother say, "and he is your grandson. As for looks, people stare at him because he is so beautiful. Where in this city of Takarazuka would you find a more beautiful boy? What, would you prefer him to look like some of his schoolmates who resemble badgers?"

Minoru had sneaked back to the garden to weep frustrated tears in silence. He was filled with questions about his father, but experience had taught him that to ask anyone brought more tears from his mother, more hot words between the grandparents. He learned that it was best to wonder in silence and wait, hoping for a better understanding of things.

Maybe, he thought, turning the packet over and over in his hands, *maybe at last grandfather will speak to me from the grave.*

He rose from the cushion, picking it up to be carried into the house. Carefully he slid the glass doors together and bolted them shut for the night. Going up the stairs to his bedroom, he turned off all the lights as he went. Once in his room, he turned on the light above his desk and sat before it with his head in his hands. Here he was free to give way to his grief. Great tears rolled unheeded from his eyes and dropped upon the blotter on his desk. When his grief was spent, and the hurt in his chest had eased from acute pain to heaviness, he took the packet again in his hands and began to untie the cord.

2

MINORU UNTIED the string which held the packet and emptied its contents upon the desk top. He sat for a few minutes looking at the things scattered there as if wondering where to start first in looking them over. Slowly he began to assort them, pushing them into different stacks before him.

He first picked up the kodak pictures bound with a rubber band and eagerly shuffled through them looking to see, if by chance, there should be a picture of his father. There was no such picture; most of them were of himself in different stages of his childhood. Without further interest, he bound them again with the band and put them aside.

A bunch of legal papers with the name and address of his lawyer under the rubber band was the next packet he picked up; then deciding that these could wait he put them back into the packet. One or two of his more than excellent school reports were there. It was so like his grandfather to have kept those. At the very bottom of the stack there was a long envelope addressed to him. Minoru's hands trembled as he broke the seal and drew out many sheets of thin writing paper filled with his grandfather's carefully brushed characters. Looking at the writing, Minoru remembered how his grandfather had tried to teach him the fine art of writing with a brush. It had not worked, for Minoru had his own particular style of writing and had stubbornly stuck to it. His grandfather, disgusted with him, had given up trying to teach him in the Japanese manner.

Minoru unfolded the letter carefully and held the pages under the light.

March 22

Minoru Tada:

Today I paid another visit to the doctor. He found my trouble to be cancer of the liver and told me the facts frankly. He supposes that there are only a few more months of life for me; I know within myself that he is right. I am not telling you or Obasan for it would only make your days too heavy with sorrow and waiting. You would be powerless to help so it is best for me to carry this thing alone, bearing my pain and heaviness of spirit in the true Japanese way.

Each day, as I have the strength, I shall write of things about which I could not bring myself to speak. My feelings about them are too deep; I cannot speak to you of them without tears. You have never seen me cry, have you?

Often, I am sure, you have misunderstood me. There have

been times when I did not understand myself. I was always disappointed that our only child was a girl, your mother. I wanted a son.

My greatest disappointment came in 1939 when your mother by chance met an American doctor, who was in Japan for a while doing some kind of research. She kept meeting him without our knowledge and before we were aware of it she found herself with child by this man. Before she knew this herself, the doctor had departed our shores to return to America. I never saw the man. Had I seen him, I am sure that I should have killed him in my extreme bitterness. Never had such a disgrace come to our old and honorable family.

Minoru had to stop reading here to dry his tears. He had never experienced such turmoil of soul, such intense hate. Until this minute his father had been a mystical, shadowy someone from nowhere. Now he knew the truth: he was an American — an American doctor who had used his little mother and cast her aside like an orange which was sucked dry.

Minoru found himself beating his fists on the desk top in his passion. "I'll track down that fox if I have to spend my life doing it, and when I have found him, I'll even the score with him." This he promised aloud to the room between his hoarse sobs. For a long while he sat unmoving at the desk with his head upon his folded arms. Now and again his shoulders heaved with wracking sobs. When he grew more quiet, he picked up the letter to continue reading.

Before you were born, I arranged a marriage for your mother with a Mr. Tada from Kyushu Island. He knew that she was with child by a foreigner, but the large sum of money that I gave as a bonus, made everything right with him. I got what I bargained for — a name for you. The bargain also removed the hated sight of your mother from our home.

It was then my intention to adopt a son to carry on the Takahashi name, but your grandmother set herself against that, so I did not carry through against her wishes.

When you were born, and proved to be so foreign in appearance, Tada, the rascal, wanted to back down on his part of the bargain. Already your mother was sick with unhappiness and begged constantly to be allowed to come back to us, even to be a servant in our home. At first I refused. Then your grandmother became ill and needed her daughter. Everyone was unhappy. It was a terrible time. Finally I agreed to your mother's coming back to us only if she would consent to putting you in an orphanage. I offered to pay such a place to keep you. Your mother refused. Things ended in a terrible snarl. At last one day, Tada brought your mother and you to Takarazuda and left you at our gate. I was forced to take you in.

You were almost a year old when you came to live with us. For months I refused to look at you. I hated the sight of your queer looking face, beautiful though you certainly were. Your grandmother loved you from the first and saw nothing except good in you. Because of my attitude, she was harsh with me.

Try to understand this thing from my point of view, Minoru, and judge me not harshly at this time. For a time I was crushed by the disgrace of the thing, though looking back, I might have struggled a bit harder in the situation and thought less about myself and wounded pride.

Who can resist the love of an innocent baby? When you began to toddle about the house you had eyes for only me. You never noticed my repulsion for you but dogged my footsteps from morning until night. You loved me more than you loved your mother and grandmother. They could not understand it; neither could I.

Your love was like an acorn in a crack of a wall. Once an acorn begins to swell, even a rock wall gives way before its unyielding force. So it was with you — an acorn in my cracked heart. I had no strength to resist you. No matter how hard I tried to be stern with you, in a few minutes you were back, forgiving me, and loving me just the same. You trailed me everywhere; you became my little shadow.

I have told you all of this to help explain to you many things: My stout resistance against all things foreign to Japan. It seemed to me then, and it seems to me now, that the flood of Western ways which have swept our land after the war are changing our people. Whether for our good or not, time must tell.

I now have no strength to fight anything, so I try not to think of my country's future. As an onlooker, I look at the seeming madness abroad in our land and wonder where it will lead us.

Always, I tried to train you in the strict Japanese way. My efforts were not always successful. I could feel you pulling off in a different direction.

I am glad that you were too young to remember the awful years of war. When war-hysteria swept our land and the military leaders tried to make us believe that it was our god-given task to rule all of Asia, I, for one, never believed it. All around us there were people who did. Sensible people lost their power to think or reason.

Knowing that my country would need steel, I buried myself in helping to produce it. (I made money during the war — that is the reason I can now leave you a well-to-do young man.)

Even though I hated everything American, because of the accident of your birth, I knew that we had committed harakiri when we gave the dastardly stroke to their navy at Pearl Harbor. We should not have done that, and it was the beginning of our undoing. Until then our victories in the East had been phenomenal.

Once the American forces were rallied against us, it was only a matter of time before our defeat. Those years for me were filled with hate; I hated war, I hated Americans who were rich and powerful, I hated our Japanese war-mongers who hood-winked the people and catapulted us into war.

When our Emperor was forced to announce ignominious defeat to his subjects in 1945, I felt that the end of the world had come for us as a nation. Life was never the same for me again.

You were only five years old when the war ended. When you entered kindergarten that year, our troubles were multiplied. Your playmates taunted you with your difference in appearance, and at every taunt your mother died a little more. You were in the second grade when her frail body simply gave out. Your grandmother and I were then your only family, and I began to try to make up for some of the wrongs I had done you in the past. I hope you do not remember any of them.

Except for the strange blood which courses through your veins I would not, if I could, change you in any way. You have been a dutiful boy, a brilliant student and a worthy heir. I could not have asked for better. As your grandmother often reminded me, the only thing that I disliked about you was the thing for which you could in no way be blamed. She was straight in her thinking; I was wrong in mine. I confess it to you here. Please forgive me.

Much has already changed in Japan — my Japan. Things which seemed to have mattered so much to me at one time seem of little consequence now. All of our national barriers are down. Airplanes now span our oceans, our language has been reduced to a learnable one for foreigners who have invented systems of their own for mastering it. During this time of great change much will be lost; much gained. Who can say for better or for worse? Already there is a prosperity here which we have not known before. People eat better, dress better and are more aware that they belong to a world not entirely Japanese.

Now, Minoru, you know why I never wanted you to be a doctor. Because of your American father I hated not only all Americans, but all doctors as well. But, in this final illness I have been forced to rethink that attitude, for I have come to have great respect for the doctors who are able to keep me from pain.

If you still have the desire to become a doctor, I withdraw my objection. There will be sufficient money for you to train in Japan; even in America if that should be your desire. You have a fine mind, my son, and more than average good looks, and you have American blood coursing through your veins. I leave no directives for you, for who can know what is best? You alone can decide the direction for your life.

My life is closing in upon me as the darkness used to fold in upon the garden on summer evenings. I know, now that it is too late, that I have done too much hating in my life. I know, too, how often my will has been pushed aside by circumstances beyond my control — circumstances strange and hateful to me.

Now that the end is near, I have been wondering if hate has had something to do with this illness. When you become a doctor, look into this angle to see if there may be some grounds for my thinking.

There is so much that we do not know about life and the business of living. At least I have learned something about hate and its power to cripple a man's life. I have learned something too about the power of love. You taught me that during your babyhood. I know that pure love can melt hate. So after learning all that this letter reveals to you, Minoru, keep hate from your heart. It only makes one hard and it bars one from happiness and contentment. It dwarfs one's very soul. This I know.

I leave you, my son and heir, with deep regret.

Your grandfather,
Takahashi, Ichijiro

For a time Minoru sat with his head in his hands. The emotional upheaval caused by the letter, adding a strain to that of the past few days, seemed almost too much to be borne. He wondered if he had enough strength to get himself to bed, then noticed with appreciation that Obasan had laid out his futons.

He wearily reached for the canvas bag to replace the scattered contents when from it fell a card with a snapshot attached with a paper clip. He looked first at the card — David M. McLean, M.D. — it read. There was the name of a Medical Center in Cleveland, Ohio, beneath the name.

As lightning splits the heavens with its forked streaks of fire, so a streak of remembering flashed into Minoru's mind. DAVID!

"Dabido, Dabido," he could hear his mother murmuring to him when he used to lie half asleep in her arms, cuddled against her warm breast. Sometimes in the daytime, when they were alone in their room she would say to him, "Let's pretend that your name is Dabido, and you call me Chōchō San."

Minoru had been old enough to know that Chōchō meant butterfly, but Dabido he did not know. He did not like the sound of it so he had refused to play the game.

"Dabido," was David in Japanese. He hurriedly detached the picture and under the light scanned it greedily. His mother, then a beautiful slim girl dressed in kimona was standing beneath the blossoming cherry trees. Beside her stood a tall American man — his father — David M. McLean, M.D. Minoru reached for his magnifying glass, used in the study of Chinese characters, and studied the face of the smiling American man. Minoru saw something of his own face there in the picture: the same broad brow, the same wave in his hair and eyes well-spaced in a pear-shaped face.

"These are my parents," he heard his voice saying aloud. "These two brought me into being. This man fathered me and does not know that I exist."

Minoru wept again in an anguish never known to him before. Swirls of hate shook him, his head swam with the rush of blood, and tears of anger fell upon the desk. All the evil things he had ever heard about American soldiers somehow centered in this one American smiling so happily in the photograph. He flung the picture back into the packet. He left them on his desk and tumbled into his bed, exhausted.

3

MINORU ROLLED OVER on his futon bed and tried to decide where he was. Things seemed so strange to him. He was unable to locate himself in time or place. As the familiar objects of the room began to take shape in his blurred vision, he remembered that it was the day after his grandfather's funeral and the earthquaking experience of the night. He was weak with frustration and grief.

He lay for a long while looking up at the ceiling trying to assort his jumbled thoughts. Finally he reached from his bed to slide back the shoji (paper doors) which separated his room from the balcony. The sun was high in the heavens; he had slept the clock around. He could not remember ever having stayed in bed so late; he was never allowed to sleep late. His grandfather, an early riser himself, had seen to it that his household was up with him to greet a new day.

Today was different. There was no grandfather to wake him or be displeased that the servants did not wake him. All life would now be different.

The revelations concerning himself made everything strange to Minoru on this August morning. Instead of knowing *who* he was, Minoru felt a greater state of confusion. The picture of his father had made him realize for the first time that he was a part of two distinct worlds. Of course, *now* he was Japanese but he began to wonder if it would be possible to develop the other side of himself.

The letter had broken the facts too abruptly for him. Without his grandfather's heavy hand of authority, he felt helpless and unequal to the demands which would be made of him. In the past, there had been times when he had strained against the bars of the old man's will, but never once had he rebelled. Now that the bars were removed, and he was left free and alone, he was frightened as he tried to look into the future.

There were decisions to be made right away. Permission had been granted for him to follow medicine as a profession if he so desired it. Now, since he had discovered that the man who was his father was a doctor, he was not sure that he wanted that. There was the lawyer to be visited to learn how he stood financially. Since he was only eighteen years of age, the lawyer would perhaps be his guardian for the next few years, and there were other responsibilities to be shouldered. "Am I equal to it?" he asked himself.

He continued to lie on his futon, looking over the tops of the dwarfed trees in the garden visible through the opened doors.

He heard Obasan begin to stir in the kitchen shortly after he had opened the doors. Soon she appeared bringing his breakfast on a tray. This she did every morning. His grandfather had permitted it, since it gave him an extra hour to review his lessons for the day, before going to school. The smell of the hot miso soup was strengthening to him as Obasan entered with his tray and spoke her good morning.

"I did nothing in the house this morning until I knew you were awake," she smilingly told him. "I know how much you need to sleep after the past strenuous days. Since there is now no school, there is no reason why you should not take more rest."

As the old woman said this, Minoru knew that, in her way, she too had strained against the iron bars of authority. It was slightly shocking to realize that this was so of Obasan as well as himself.

Minoru smiled at her, and said nothing. She continued to chatter on, "I went into the garden to putter about a bit, so that even my footsteps in the house would not disturb you. Rest is good for you, and you must take advantage of this vacation period."

"Obasan, please set the tray on the desk. I shall use that until I can get a table in here," he told her.

Obasan set the tray on the desk as he had requested, but this sudden change of things did not go unmarked by her. She watched him as he got out of his covers, drew his kimona close about his body and tied the sash as he walked to seat himself before the tray.

With her own thoughts safe-hidden in her mind she lifted the futons still warm with his body heat, out to the balcony to spread them in the hot sunshine. Now, except for the disarray of his clothes, the room was in order, and the young master could eat his breakfast in peace.

"It's a beautiful day," she said to Minoru, who glanced again at the golden sunshine flooding the great out-of-doors, and nodded his agreement; his mouth was too full of food for verbal answer. When he had washed it down with a swallow of hot soup, he asked her, "Are you going to be very busy this morning, Obasan?"

"Not so busy. While your grandfather lay ill, I had time to thoroughly clean the house. My work now will be lighter through the hot days. Is there something you'd like for me to do for you?"

"Yes, there is," Minoru answered hesitatingly. "When you have finished your breakfast, please come back up here for a sōdan (talk). There are some things I wish to ask you, some questions which only you can answer."

"Of course, Minoru," the old servant answered and quickened her pace to get accomplished the task yet awaiting her hands.

When she returned to his room, she found him dressed, seated on a zabuton with his feet folded beneath him. Another cushion had been placed opposite him on the straw floor. He motioned her to be seated as she entered.

He waited in silence while she smoothed her kimona over her knees and folded her legs neatly beneath her body. *Like a sea gull lighting on the water,* Minoru thought, as he watched her.

With her work-worn hands folded sedately in her lap, she waited for him to speak that which was on his mind.

"There are just the two of us now, Obasan," he said, barely holding back his tears.

"It is so, Minoru, but soon you will be of age to bring an Oyome (bride) here to this house of your fathers'. Again there will be laughter and life because there will be children. Years pass so quickly. This year you will enter college. It seems such a short time since you were a baby yourself."

"All that will be years away, Obasan," Minoru blushingly told her. "There will be at least three years of college, and if I decide to study to be a doctor there will be yet more years of study."

At his mention of studying medicine, Obasan took a deep breath. She well knew what his grandfather had thought of that idea, so she kept her thoughts to herself. She was thinking, *There will be change! Already this morning his breakfast on the desk while he sat in his chair to eat it, now this talk of medical school which his grandfather ruled against, but, each must go his own way, and Minoru must go it alone. Each must choose for himself. This is New Japan.*

"The packet of papers you handed me last night contained a long letter from Ojiisan." Before he could say more, the old woman cut in, "Yes, I know. I saw him writing, writing, writing, many days during his illness."

"In it he told me many things — things that I had never known before." Minoru waited for some comment from her; there was none.

"First, Obasan, I want to ask, will you stay with me, or would you prefer going back to your family?"

"I have no family but you, Minoru. Where else could I go? This is home to me now. If it is your desire for me to stay, here is where I'd prefer to remain."

"Good," Minoru said with evident relief. "I hoped you'd want to stay with me. We'll carry on together as always. I can't remember when you were not a part of the family, Obasan. I have never thought to ask about your family for I've always considered you a part of ours."

"My husband was a soldier, Minoru, and one of the first to be shipped to Manchuria in the days before the war. He was killed there. We had only one son. During the days that fire bombs were rained upon Kobe, I was at the vegetable shop when one made a direct hit upon our house. Our son, nine years old, was sleeping there after his return from school. He, the house, everything went up in flames! Here at your grandfather's house I found a home — and peace through work."

When she saw the sorrow in his eyes, she brightened a bit, and said quickly, "War is a terrible thing. It is hard on everybody —

those who lose, those who win. It is the way man has always acted! I don't know why. I lost everything, so did millions of others. Something of oneself dies too, but the body lives on. I have known sorrow and loss, too, Minoru."

Looking at the servant seated before him with her face as wrinkled as an apple left in the sun, Minoru had a desire to weep for all the sorrows which beset the world — weep as he had wept the night before, but he managed to control himself.

Minoru unfolded his grandfather's letter, opening it upon the straw floor, pressing it flat with his hand. "In this letter," he spoke softly to her, "Grandfather spoke to me from the grave."

"Yes, I know. Much he should have told you while he was living, but it wasn't his way. You must not hold it against him, Minoru. He was really not a hard man. I shall answer all the questions which you ask of me, but it would have been better for the answers to have come from him."

"Most of my questions, Obasan, have to do with my mother and her relations with the man who is my father." This was said more frankly than a Japanese would have said it, Obasan thought, but she sat waiting until a direct question should be asked of her before she spoke.

Minoru held out to her the picture of the American man and his mother. "Did you ever see this man, Obasan?"

"No, I never did, neither did your grandparents. Michiko met him one day at the theater in Takarazuka. After their first meeting, she managed to keep seeing him in secret; this she told me long after you were born."

The old woman brought the snapshot close to her nearsighted eyes and tried to get a clearer sight of the man in question.

"In the packet you gave me last night, I found that clipped to this name card."

"Yes, I know. After your mother became nothing, I found this hidden in her room and gave it to your grandfather."

"Was the man's name Dabido Makurein?" Minoru asked giving the Japanese pronunciation.

"Hai (yes), or so it sounded to me. Michiko used to talk to me about him in secret. When you were born, Michiko gave you the name Dabido Minoru Tada. But, when she brought you here to live, the Master would not have it. He cut the Dabido from your name."

"Obasan, what illness killed my mother? I only remember that she was sick a long time. In fact, it seems to me now that she was always sick."

"Michiko was never well after the Americans left Japan. The doctors said that she had lung-sickness, but I always knew it was of the heart. She loved that Makurein San, Minoru. She loved him very much."

Minoru sat fighting back the angry tears. At last he said, "What became of the man, Tada, whose name I bear?"

"After your mother came back here to live, we never saw the man again. But now," she said knowingly, "now that you are your grandfather's heir, I dare say he will show up some day." She said this with the knowing toss of her head which Minoru had connected with her wise ways since childhood. It now gave him something new to think about. The old servant knew much about the human race. She probably was right in her conjecture about Mr. Tada.

4

FOR SEVERAL DAYS Minoru lingered about the house; sat in the garden in the sunshine, thinking over all the things which had been revealed to him in a heap, trying to absorb and come to grips with them.

Nothing seemed right without the overpowering presence of his grandfather. No matter where he turned in these days, the spirit of the old man seemed to cling to the home surroundings like the smell of upturned earth.

Questions about life, death, the purpose of it all, swarmed his torn mind. To whom should he turn for answers? Only once in his life had he questioned his grandfather about such matters. It had been shortly after his grandmother's death. "Ojiisan," he remembered asking, "where are Mother and Grandmother now? Where did they go after they died?"

"S-a-a-a," his grandfather, an ardent Buddhist, said, then sat smoking his long pipe in meditative silence, "perhaps to some higher existence — some higher state — at least that is our hope."

Though Minoru found this answer confusing rather than helpful, he made no comment but to himself he said, "Perhaps — perhaps — a rather gray stretch if one pauses to look down it." Never again had he tried to draw his grandfather into a discussion of such things.

Twice in his life he had gone with Ojiisan to visit temples in Kyoto. The first time he was still a small boy with alert eyes for everything. As they had entered the giant gates of the temple Nishi

(West) Honganji, the richest and largest of the ancient temples in the historical city, walked across the expanse of the cream-colored pebbles of the wide courtyard and entered the gloomy recesses of the main hall, the old man had kept up a stream of instructions for him.

"Notice the immensity of this place, Minoru. Look up at those ceiling carvings above the Amida Nyorai. They are hundreds of years old and are now priceless. These Chinese carvings date back to the seventeenth century — to the T'ang Period."

Not one single building, garden or sliding door of the rooms and corridors with paintings by the famous masters of their day, escaped Ojiisan's notice or comment. He paused in his progress through the great temple to contemplate the famous Chinese landscapes on the doors of the Abbott's Audience chamber: painted wisteria, bamboo branches and sparrows — the work of Maruyama in mid-eighteenth century.

Minoru's young head swam with it all, and, even after having seen his grandfather in his act of worship — clapping his hands before the statue, reciting over and over "Namu Amida Butsu" — Minoru felt that it was all play-acting and without real meaning. He kept these thoughts to himself, however; since then he had, time and again, turned them over in his mind to ponder and question.

Again, when he was fourteen, he had gone with the old man to Higashi (East) Honganji for the celebration of the anniversary of the death of the founder of the Shin sect of Buddhism. The memory of the great pageant had stamped itself upon his young mind: the procession of monks dressed in their dazzling brocades as they marched among the multitudes who crowded the temple courts and spilled out into the street.

Even now, when he tried, Minoru could recall the spine-tingling notes of the high-pitched bamboo flutes blown by the monks as they marched along. They had stood in the broiling midday sun to watch a dance before the Hall of Prayer, armed monks fighting for their lives against demons who were bent on destroying them. Minoru remembered how enthralled his grandfather had been, and how bored he had been with it all.

As Minoru recalled these things, he had to admit, that, through his own devotion to this complex and confused religion, Ojiisan had managed to evolve for himself a way of life. He had managed to instill into his grandson Filial Piety — one of the supreme virtues of Buddhists. Thinking of this, Minoru, now the head of the house of Takahashi, wondered how it would be possible for him to pass on such teachings to those who would carry on the family — if he knew nothing of them himself.

He decided that it was his duty to get himself informed in the ways of Buddhism so that he could at least give proper honors to the dead. This could best be done, he decided, by visiting the temples of Kyoto and by interviewing some priest who could guide him in his studies.

So, his first trip away from home after his period of mourning was to the great historical city of Kyoto, an hour's ride by fast train from Takarazuka. On his way to the railway station a feeling of well-being flooded his young mind and body. Looking about at the flow of life around him, he knew that he had been missed not at all; but the fact stood, he had missed it. He thought how nice it would be to have school start again. Then his time would be scheduled. There was a pleasant rhythm about scheduled time — the only way he had ever lived it. He was looking forward to the mental challenge which college would bring to him. He wondered, as he walked along, whether his choice of Kwansai University had been the wise choice if he really intended to study medicine. Perhaps it would have been wiser to have entered Kyoto University for college, then to have followed through to medicine. He had made his choice because Kwansai University was nearest his home, then, too, there were many Canadians and Americans on the faculty there. They could open windows upon a world which rightly belonged to him. These were things he could think about at a later time, so he pushed them aside.

As the train hurtled toward Kyoto he began to feel within himself a surge of freedom. After all, he rightly belonged to two worlds, and there was no reason why he could not work to know them both. He had never had his grandfather's aversion to America. Now that he knew his roots ran to that far-off country, he felt a sudden claim to the place about which he was woefully ignorant.

Looking about him, Minoru began to realize for the first time how much of the Western World had flowed into Japan since the war. He only knew the post-war years and was therefore a product of New Japan. His grandfather had not hesitated to use electricity, to ride electric trains, to wear foreign clothes or to ride in taxis — yet these were all channeled into Japan from the West. Even the modern machinery, which his grandfather's company used in the manufacture of steel, was machinery imported from the West. There was much along this line to be thought out, Minoru concluded, but the sudden stopping of the train at Kyoto station cut short his thoughts.

When the train door slid open, Minoru rushed through it with all the others, out upon the platform already swarming with humanity.

Suddenly the idea of visiting temples and priests no longer appealed to him. Here he was in the interesting old city with a whole unplanned day before him. Never in his life had he been allowed to spend an idle, aimless day.

As suddenly as the thought struck him, just as suddenly he decided to give himself over to the impulses of the moment and to squander the day at will. As he walked along the streets in the warm sunshine, the experience proved exhilarating to him. It was as if he were seeing Old Japan for the first time. During the war years, because Kyoto held so many of the relics and priceless ancient treasures, it had been declared an open city. *Here,* Minoru thought, *is Old Japan — my grandfather's Japan — in minature.* He took his time in his progression about the city, consciously weighing values in the light of the new age, drawing his own conclusions about things in general.

Heretofore, his mind had run only in channels set by his superiors: teachers, grandfather and neighbors. Now he was free to think and make decisions for himself. He found this to be a heady experience on this August day. Throwing back his shoulders, he said almost aloud, "I am a person — an entity — distinct and different. My life is before me; I can live it as I please." Always until this moment he had smarted at the "difference"; today was a new turn in his road. His full six feet of height, his more than average good looks, his solid ability as a student were things which he added up in his mind to find the scales of fortune weighted in his favor.

After this unusual bit of introspection, he deliberately turned his thoughts to the things about him. He had never seen so many kimona-dressed women in his life. In the new freedom-years, women of Japan, for the most part, had donned yōfuku (foreign style dress). Measuring the new mode of dress against these flowing garments of Old Japan, he found that he liked the new style better.

He smiled to think how his currents of thought were running contrary to those of his grandfather's. Somehow in the aura of his new-found freedom, it did not matter greatly since Ojiisan could no longer walk beside him. Much that his grandfather had discarded as bad, Minoru began to see made good sense. He could enjoy and appreciate his grandfather's Japan, but never again would he accept a thing because another person said that he must. He had subconsciously rejected the idea of visiting the temples for this reason. He was not blindly committed to follow the Buddhist thought because his forefathers had done so. There might be a better way. If so, he'd like to be left free to search for it, he decided.

As he returned home that night, after the memorable day, he swung up the familiar alley with a new stride and with new purpose in his steps.

After the good supper Obasan had prepared for him, he went to sit on the upstairs balcony looking down the alley upon the bright lights of Takarazuka. This was his home city, but it was really unknown to him. The great theater district, now ablaze with lights, was a closed door to him. In former years, when he had expressed a desire to attend the performances, Ojiisan had cut him short. Now he knew that it was there that his mother had met the strange man, so it was a despised place in the old man's mind. Someday he would go down to see it for himself, Minoru decided.

My life is now my own. My ambitions are my affair. There is plenty of money to follow through with all plans that I may choose to make. These thoughts almost sang in his mind.

He left the balcony to go into his room. Seating himself at the desk, he took out a notebook and pencil, and with them he began to make notes of the thoughts which were filling his mind.

1. I must act as a distinct person, but I must take responsibilities for my own actions.
2. I must not completely forget my grandfather's teachings; neither must I follow them blindly without weighing them for myself.
3. I must at all times be loyal to myself.
4. I must chart my way carefully through life. Once I have charted, I must follow through at all cost.

Here he paused. "Chart my way." How does one chart one's way in a life that cannot be counted on to run according to plan? "Hateful circumstances" is what his grandfather had said caused the stumbling blocks in one's way. How does one know which of two ways is better?

There was that matter of seeking revenge on his despised father. *How can I tell where that would lead? Is it right that I should desire such a thing even though the man did ruin my mother's life?* While he was thinking these thoughts his grandfather's words came to him, "Try not to hate, Minoru — try not to hate."

Suddenly Minoru knew that he was exhausted after such an unusual day, and after an evening spent in introspection. He knew now that sleep was the only thing for which he really longed at the moment.

5

MINORU HAD NOW BEEN a University student five months. From his first day of getting adjusted to the new situations incident to college life, he had been intrigued with all the promises of wider horizons he sensed about him. Most of all he was pleased with the final decision to attend Kwansai University.

There was a decided foreign look about the place — the great sprawling, tree-spotted campus, buildings of Western design standing about the huge quadrangle. These had been built long before the wave of foreign newness struck Japan.

In the New Japan, quickly raised from the ashes of the war years, these types of steel and concrete buildings were the accepted thing. They gave to the rebuilt cities a new and substantial look.

On this cold December day, as Minoru stood at the front gate of the campus, waiting for the three friends who made the daily train trip with him to and from Takarazuka, he turned to face the main building of the college. He looked with new appreciation upon the grace of its structure and thought again of his utter good fortune to be among the teeming thousands who came here each day, seeking training for life. Here he was finding challenge in every course, an experience new for him.

Minoru was finding college life more strenuous as well as more challenging. In his high school days, he had been able to get out of bed at a decent hour in the morning, eat a leisurely breakfast, then make his way across the hard-packed path across the paddy field to the river. There, on the river road he would join the teeming morning life — the bustle of it never ceased to fascinate him. Life currents seemed to have flowed about him on all sides. The river was a highway of commerce with a bustle all its own.

During those school days, if he walked fast, he could be at his desk in twenty minutes after leaving home. Now, as one among the multitudes of Japanese college students in the country, he joined the push and shove as a commuter on the jam-packed fast lines which shuttled back and forth in the overcrowded country. At first it irked Minoru to be forced to keep the strict time schedule of a train. He hated the crush of it all and the rudeness displayed by fellow students; but, in a matter of weeks, he had learned to look out for himself, to push and shove with the best of them, for a few inches of standing space in the trains.

Each day, after the struggle of train travel, there were more strenuous strivings to get a toe-hold on one of the crowded busses which dumped the thousands of students at the university gate. However, it did not take him long to accustom himself to the discomforts, and to accept it all as a way of student life to be endured without complaint.

Before he entered college, he had made a final decision to study medicine. There was no struggle now since his grandfather had withdrawn his objection to the idea. Had his grandfather lived and held to his objections, he still would have made the choice no matter what the cost. He was, however, grateful that there was nothing to hold him back.

As the days came and went, Minoru felt the tight bands of Ojiisan's authority grow limp and fall from him like broken thongs. Along with the slackening bonds, he felt a sudden surge of freedom. Until now, when he was free to make his own choices, he had not felt the full constriction of the old man's authority.

With such thoughts in his mind, he threw back his shoulders and sucked into his lungs the fresh, frosty air of December. There was a taste of snow in it. He watched the dry leaves slithering along the path and wondered why his friends were so long in coming.

He had met these boys on his first day of traveling to the university. Each day, after that, they made it a habit to take the return trip to Takarazuka together. These daily visits on the trains made the trip enjoyable. His daily association with Masao, Eiji, and Toshio had been a new venture in friendship for him. Until now, his association with boys his own age had been restricted to the school playground in supervised play. After school it had always been required of him that he return home to help Ojiisan with the multitudinous duties which the old man could think up. Minoru had never questioned the fairness of it; he obeyed without question, but he had missed the carefree play with other boys.

Thinking of this now, Minoru knew that all the while Ojiisan had been trying to shield him from the slurs and sneers of his fellow students. He wondered now if most of that had been only in his grandfather's mind. Here in college he had felt nothing of the imagined slights. No one seemed to notice that he was different. Among the student throng, he had noticed others like himself with a strangeness about them, even though they seemed unconscious of the difference.

He looked up to see his three friends swinging along the walk toward him. Soon they were in the bus clinging to the straps. Masao looked over to see Minoru bowed to protect his head from the low bus top, "Minoru, do you like being so tall?" he asked.

"I never think about it until I get in places like this," Minoru goodnaturedly answered. "It can be an advantage in the train looking over the heads of people to find an empty spot, but here, and at home where all of our doors are too low, I am continually getting knocked in the head when I forget to stoop." The grimace he made at the memory of the blows on his defenseless head made all about him burst into laughter.

"You are not the least awkward, Minoru," Eiji said. "Perhaps your tennis playing has helped you there. Do you dance, Minoru?"

"No," Minoru answered quickly, "I've never danced." To his mind came a mental picture of the traditional Japanese dance, slow movements of the hands, sudden jerks of the head and posing of the feet.

"Some day you must come with us to the dance hall. There they will teach you to dance the modern way — with girls. I have learned, and I like it."

Minoru had no comment on this revolutionary idea. Except for his mother, his grandmother and Obasan he had had absolutely no contact with the opposite sex.

His grandfather had taken great pains to keep before him the facts of his own wedding and all the events leading up to it. "Not once did I see my wife, your grandmother, before our wedding day. See how happy your grandmother and I are? Japan's way is best. This falling in love the Western way — it is not good and no good comes of it. It is best to fall in love *afterwards.* Parents and go-betweens know best for the young. Remember that, Minoru, when your times comes to choose a yome san (bride)."

By the time his grandmother was dead, and Minoru was in his teens, he learned the one reason it worked so well for the Japanese man was the freedom allowed him in his choice of a mistress or a favorite geisha. No questions were ever asked by the wife. Minoru learned that this was *not* his grandfather's way. He could speak from his own experience, his marriage *had* been a good one. *But then,* Minoru thought, *my grandmother was a real person, and she reserved always the right to speak her mind on a matter. That certainly is not usual in the average Japanese household.*

When Ojiisan managed to work in this lecture, it was his habit to deliver his opinions, then sit back on his heels waiting for some comment from this strange youth who happened to be his grandson. Minoru always sat unmoving, giving neither approval nor disapproval to the ideas expressed. The fact was that the idea of marriage had never touched him. He would not trouble the idea until the moment it came to trouble him. Even in his early teens, he knew if his grandfather were living, when that time came there would be no choice for him, so why speak about the matter? There were too many plans to be worked through before he would be forced to come to grips with marriage. He never entered into an argument with his grandfather; experience had taught him the wisdom of silence.

When Minoru listened to these new-found friends who often discussed such things, he gathered that each of them looked forward to the new freedom which had come after the army of occupation. Each fully intended choosing his own wife. There were, however, problems even in freedom, Minoru gathered from listening to his friends.

"It is not an easy thing to go about getting to know a girl well enough to fall in love. If you so much as ask one to go out with you for an evening, in *her* mind you are as good as engaged to her," Masao said, then told them the story of a friend who had gotten himself ensnared by one lone dinner date. "It's really frightening. I have asked only one girl out for dinner in all my life. That's enough for me!"

"The same here," Eiji admitted, "The girl misunderstood my intentions and I had a terrible time explaining why I invited another girl for another date. It was sticky business getting disentangled from her *and* her mother. Never again! But how can I ever get to know a girl well enough to ask her to be my wife?"

"I have a solution," Minoru told them laughing, "why not engage a go-between to do the running back and forth, weighing matters, matching dispositions, finances and physical characteristics? That is what I shall do. It can't be all bad; it has been working in Japan for centuries." His joking manner made his friends laugh heartily, for this sounded incongruous coming from one who was not truly Japanese. It was a continual puzzle to them that this half-westerner, as was plain for anyone to see, should be the most conservative in his way of thinking.

"It worked for centuries because the Japanese woman had nowhere to turn when she came to the age for marrying. What else could she do?" Toshio asked them. "Today it is different. The girls are being educated, all professions are wide open to them and they can plan their lives as we do. They can even inherit property along with their brothers and are not now always dependent upon their males. It makes a difference, and we might as well face the fact — the *hard* fact."

"All that you say is true, Toshio," Eiji said quickly, "but just the same girls today are in a panic for fear they will be left out while the marriage wheel is in motion. In the olden days, all a girl had to do to get married was to keep breathing. That is not so today; they are more or less on their own and it frightens them. The new way may be a better system but I'm beginning to doubt it. There ought to be a middle course of the old and new combined. I have sisters, you know, and I hear much discussion from their side of this thing."

Before the three friends separated, they discussed plans for the holidays.

"Why" Minoru asked, "are these days referred to as *Christmas Holidays?*"

"S-a-a-a," Eiji emitted, "maybe it is because so many of our faculty are Christians. The University, you know, was begun by Christian missionaries; they set the pattern of holidays. Their Christmas falls about the same time as our Shogatsu (New Year), so it is all the same."

"I don't care what they call the holidays," Masao said grinning from ear to ear, "just so we have them. My folks are letting me go to Nagano Ken for skiing as soon as the snows fly. Do you ski, Minoru?"

"No," he confessed, "I've never even stood up on skiis. During the vacation I shall practice on the slopes of Mt. Rokko. Next year I'll be ready to take off with you to the Alps."

When Minoru separated from his friends and started the walk home alone, he realized that he had quickly concocted the story about skiing. It was a brand new idea, but it might not prove a bad pastime for him this year. He had also promised to go to a foreign restaurant with his friends one day soon — that too would be a new experience. What would those three friends think if they could know that he had never once held a knife or fork in his hands? He resolved to go slowly, observe carefully and learn fast. No one need know that he had had little touch with modern Japan. So far, he was finding the new experiences extremely fascinating.

Minoru had let his friends believe that his plans for the holidays were made; in reality he had no plans. He was secretly dreading the long days of enforced idleness at home. He had little heart for the festivities such as his friends were planning, and it was too soon after his grandfather's death to join them, even if he had the heart for it. The specter of loneliness came to walk beside him, and to blow itself up to enormous proportions.

Minoru pushed these thoughts aside, and concentrated on the New Year's celebration. Obasan would take charge of that, making the hot sake and the mochi cakes for the guests. Friends of his grandfather's would be sure to come on that day. He would remember to talk it over with Obasan when he reached home.

In all the days that he had known his three friends, not one word or question had there been about the compositon of his family. In spite of the strange Occidental cast to his face, they had accepted him without any show of curiosity. Thinking of this now, it gave him renewed courage and confidence.

It is not so strange that they know nothing about my family, I know nothing of theirs either. They are full-blooded Japanese, and

I know that there is money for their families to afford a college education for them. Thinking along this line, he decided that it might be smart for him to keep them in ignorance about his personal affairs. It had been drilled into him to keep secret his private business. "It is the Japanese way," he could hear Ojiisan say to him.

Some days later this resolve on his part was strengthened by something his lawyer said to him. He found Mr. Takehito Asayama sitting at his big desk stacked to its capacity with the flotsom-jetsam of a lawyer's office. He greeted the youth warmly, and after seating him across the desk, sat a moment studying Minoru's handsome face on which the features had ceased their adolescent wandering and had settled in a permanent arrangement of positive beauty. During this interlude of silence, Minoru also studied the face of his grandfather's friend of long standing, in the light of their present relationship.

Mr. Asayama, a short man even for a Japanese, had remained seated when the tall youth approached his desk. There was a square cut to his face, a sort of chiseled look about his temples and his chin. His coal-black hair was parted meticulously in the middle of his head, adding to the already cubed look of it. A liberal sprinkling of white in his hair above the temples added distinction to his dark brown face.

Before actually opening the conversation with Minoru, the lawyer shuffled papers under his hand, then looked up with his full attention centered on the business at hand.

"You are a very young man to have such wealth put into your hands, Minoru. You are also very fortunate. With the training that your grandfather gave you, I shall not worry about the way you handle things. I meant to ask you this before, are there any relatives who may resent your good fortune, and who may try to wrest some of it from you?"

Such a thing as this had never before crossed his mind. "None that I ever heard about," he answered quickly. "My mother had no brothers or sisters; I am therefore the sole heir."

Mr. Asayama looked quickly away from Minoru's light complexioned face, and, with a visible effort, left unspoken questions which seemed to tremble on his lips.

"Are you finding your present allowance sufficient for all your needs?" he asked his ward.

"For the present I find it quite ample, thank you."

They sat for a time going over matters for which Minoru had been asked to come to the office. When that was finished, Mr. Asayama leaned back in his chair to say, "If I, as your guardian, might offer a suggestion to you, Minoru, I'd be slow about letting my contemporaries know that I have more money than they. In that way, you may have fewer friends, but they will be real, and worth having."

Minoru thanked him for this advice and acknowledged it as sound. The lawyer continued to speak, "It is never a good thing for a young man to have more than enough money for his needs. It is so easy to gather loose friends, and to slip into foolish ways simply because there is the means for them."

"My needs are very simple, really, Mr. Asayama, and I mean to keep them that way, at least until I know more about the world than I now know."

"Good, keep things like that. Do you have any idea what profession you will follow after college?" He looked searchingly into the young man's face.

"I am planning to be a doctor of medicine. My plans now project to some graduate study in the United States.

"Is that so?" the lawyer asked not so much as a question but as an objection.

"By that time, the money will be in your hands, and it will be a matter for you to decide, but I do not see the need for that. Japan now has some very fine schools of medicine. I do not see why you feel it desirable to seek training elsewhere, but, of course, that is your affair."

Then as if switching the subject by design, he said, "You will be considering marriage one of these days. I hope that I shall still be around to help you in this important step. In fact," here he hesitated slightly, then went on, "your grandfather once looked upon our youngest daughter as a possible match for you. He looked upon her with great favor, and often linked your names in conversation with me." Minoru's sudden blush made him cut short this talk. He slapped his hands down on top of his desk as if that subject might be well discussed another time. He stood to indicate that their business for the day was over. They bowed to each other in parting, and Minoru left the office.

The matter of the young daughter which the guardian had mentioned lingered in Minoru's mind as he walked along the street toward home. It was perfectly clear to him, that a foreign strain of blood and a different cast of face might easily be overlooked by the most fastidious Japanese if there were money enough to soften the difference. Minoru was definitely put on his guard by this interview. During the time spent with his lawyer he definitely surged toward manhood and began to glimpse the way the wind of fortune would blow for him.

Asayama was definitely a keen and honest man; he also was not above thinking of fringe benefits which could reach far into the future through his youngest daughter.

Minoru chuckled to himself as he strode along the river thinking his own thoughts and weighing ideas which were new and interesting.

6

MINORU WOKE to a cold, overcast day. Occasional snowflakes cut through the air as if to warn one that they could get angry and take over for an hour or so to have their pleasure with the earth. Seeing this through the panes of glass, which now replaced the rice-paper doors in his bedroom, Minoru pulled his electric blanket about his shoulders and settled deeper in his warm bed.

The Christmas and New Year holidays had not been so unpleasant as he had feared they would be. In fact, he had filled them with much activity of his own choosing. He looked appreciatively about his room now completely furnished in foreign style. He had chosen a bed to match the desk and chair purchased by his grandfather. The room boasted a table, a book case, two other chairs, and a small electric stove. Even though the winter winds howled about the house, his room was a haven of comfort hitherto unknown to him. Smiling at the imagined reaction of the old man, he wondered what Ojiisan would say if it were possible for him to step into the room for a visit.

Minoru had even expected adverse criticism from Obasan, but there had been not a word as the carpenters worked to install the glass doors or when the truck came to the door with the large pieces of furniture to be carted upstairs to his room. She had even come in, after he had arranged things to suit himself, to smile and cluck her appreciation, exclaiming her long, "Ma-a-a" at the sight of the trans-formed place.

Minoru remembered that this was the day he had promised to meet his three friends at the foreign restaurant. They were to have an early lunch, afterwards attend the Takarazuka theater for the afternoon performance.

All of this would be new for him, but old-shoe for his companions. He looked forward to it with keen anticipation, even submerged excitement.

When he tapped on the floor for Obasan, he heard her begin to stir about in the kitchen beneath his room. Soon she came puffing up the steps bearing his breakfast tray. "Ohayō, gozaimasu," she said cheerily as she placed it on the table.

"Ohayō, Obasan," he replied as he adjusted his thick padded kimona about his body and seated himself at the table facing the glass panels so that he could watch the accelerated snow spatter and sift over the garden with swirling motion.

Later, when walking through the soft down of it, he was sorry that he had not allowed himself more time to wander about the

36

city before meeting his friends. He liked to feel the sharp pricks of snow against his face.

Today, for old time's sake, he took the familiar walk across the field to the road beside the river and stopped a few minutes to watch the river men steer their barges, working too hard to feel the icy winds being channeled down the river's bed. Minoru felt the cold penetrating his overcoat and started walking again. He was glad that they planned to spend the afternoon inside the theater, rather than wandering about, as they sometimes did, when they had a bit of free time to spend together.

Eiji, Masao and Toshio were already seated at the restaurant table, when he arrived. Hot tea had been served and they were sipping it with evident enjoyment, cupping their hands about the cups for the tea's extra warmth. They had walked through the snow, too, and their faces were still ruddy and glowing from the cold. As Minoru entered, they saw him and waved. When they ordered their food, Minoru waited until all had done so, then he followed Toshio's lead with an egg omlette. That, with hot tea, fresh bread and a fruit dessert he found to his liking, and since there was only the fork and the spoon to be used, he found himself managing with surprising ease.

His friends talked as they ate. That was a new experience to Minoru. He had been trained to pay attention to eating and let conversation wait until the last swallow of tea had been taken. These friends kept up a merry chatter throughout the meal. Eiji was full of his account of the skiing trip to Nagano from which he had just returned.

"We must all plan to go next year together," he said. "It was great fun. Of course, the trip up on the train, with hundreds of others who were packing their skis along, was a nightmare. None of us got sleep with the crowd and the equipment all over the place. The girls giggled and made noises all night. They would not sleep themselves, nor let any of the rest of us."

"Girls?" Minoru asked, "What were they doing there?"

"They were going to ski, too, of course. Some of them do well at it. Didn't you know that girls ski?"

"Somehow I had not thought about it. Did the girls mix freely with the boys at the resort?" he asked innocently. The sudden burst of laughter made him catch on to what their mirth was about; his sudden blush made his light skin glow almost red.

"Very freely, too freely, I'm afraid," Eiji said thoughtfully. "If this is the new freedom for women, then I fear it is a bit *too* free. It can't be a good thing for parents to loose their hold so completely upon their naive daughters. I wonder about it, wonder if it *is* best. Our group of boys stayed together at the inn and during the evenings too. I wish there was some place in this city where we could get together for talks and games. We had such a good time at the lodge."

Minoru thought of his snug room which could serve for such a place of meeting. He hesitated to speak of it; it might prove too comfortable and the use of it might absorb too much of his study-time. He decided against mentioning it.

When they had finished eating, Minoru watched as each paid his own bill; he did likewise and swung out into the snowy street with them as they hurried toward the sprawling theater.

Minoru had often passed this way, but never had he been allowed to turn into great gates. As they walked toward the theater, his friends kept up a running stream of conversation about the operas they had seen there in the past. They knew all of the current stars and spoke of them as if they were intimates.

As he went through the gate he remembered that it was here that his parents had met. The thought was a physical impact in his stomach. *Where was my mother standing when that despised creature first saw her?* He looked quickly around as if he might, in some way, be able to recognize the spot.

Minoru knew that, just as in the Noh plays men took all the parts, here, all the parts were taken by women.

"I wonder if they will ever use both women and men characters in the plays? It seems rather ridiculous that they don't," Masao said. "In such things we Japanese are difficult to change. Other changes we take to like ducks to water. Why?" Toshio and Eiji gave their opinions on the matter.

Minoru listened to them with but half a mind. His attention was centered upon the crowd which flowed beside them in the foyer of the great theater. It was hardly a crowd that one would expect to see at such a place. He could feel the currents of excitement flowing about him. Family groups, even small children, were huddled about tables near the windows of the place, eating lunches brought along for them. Old women, who looked as worn and lowly as Obasan, were in their holiday attire, excitement etched on their faces. Clearly this was a once-a-year occasion for them. Minoru caught the eyes of some of them, and smiled at them as if he understood their excitement of the moment.

Some day, I'll bring Obasan here for a treat, if she will come, Minoru promised himself. Somewhere in the back side of his mind, he could hear Ojiisan saying, as he always did when the Takara-zuka Theater was mentioned, "It's a no-good place. Such foolishness gets into the minds of the young, and takes away their common sense and judgment."

Here it was that my mother met David M. McLean! Her common sense and judgment were certainly taken away. That's the reason Ojiisan hated this place so much.

Minoru had never felt such tangible excitement. Somewhere signals were being buzzed through the building. Crowds were flowing like dark streams in reverse up the broad stairs and into the cavernous depths of the great building. Closely following Toshio who had made all the arrangements, they entered the first balcony. The usher with his flashlight led them to the row of seats with only the iron railing between them and the gathering crowd below. Minoru did not try to talk to his friends; he was too busy watching the crowds settling in below. He was again surprised at the number of children who had been brought along to such a performance.

Folks were streaming into the seats when the buzzer sounded for the show's beginning. From the time the ornate curtains began to crumple with the tightening of ropes, Minoru sat gripping the railing before him, all eyes for the spectacle which began to unfold upon the stage: the whanging samisens, the doll-like creatures who played them, the color, the lights, the unsurpassed scenery. He was caught up in the movement and the brilliance of it all. The plot was time-worn, played and replayed the world over; lovers with mountains of difficulties strewn more or less cleverly in their ill-starred paths. There was intrigue, within their households, or wherever their paths led them. There were comic characters who played time-worn tricks to afford a light touch to the otherwise heavy plot. Minoru saw more than those things: expert lighting, breathtaking scenery, whimsical characters playing their unimportant roles seriously. For over an hour he was caught in a web of magic. He blinked hard at his friends when the performance was over and the bright lights were turned on again.

"Let's go down to the lobby to get some tea," Eiji suggested. "We have half an hour for intermission."

Minoru, who thought the performance was over asked, "What comes next?"

"The last half of the afternoon is always foreign opera. That has become very popular now. Some of them are very good, some not so enjoyable. Today is to be *Madame Butterfly*. Do you know it?"

Minoru felt, rather than saw, Toshio give Eiji a ram in his ribs with his elbow. He thought nothing of it until the play was half over, then all began to clear for him.

Back in their seats after the intermission, Minoru watched the orchestra warming up to their task in the pit. The curtain rose upon a Japanese scene in a tea house, and before any of the characters appeared, Minoru listened to the haunting strains of foreign music, the lilt of which seemed to carry him to float on a cloud. The screaming, haunting strains of the violins stirred deep emotion within him. He had heard little foreign music in his lifetime. He found himself enchanted. There were exchanged whispers among the three friends seated by him, but Minoru was too busy riveting his attention to pay attention to them.

Not until Lt. Pinkerton put in his appearance did Minoru scent the plot which was beginning to unfold upon the stage. He tried to forget the roles and to center his attention upon the male part being played by an actress. He noted how well she managed her body, her hands, her feet. Through it all, he was forced to witness the little geisha falling in love with an American man, who was to love her only for the moment. Somewhere he could hear his mother's voice, as if through the cotton wool of Time's wrapping, "You call me Chōchō San; I'll call you Dabido." Now in a flash he understood. In another age, in another setting his little mother had been the Chōchō of such a shameful play; David McLean had been in the role of Lt. Pinkerton. He understood why his friends had been apprehensive as they filed back into the theater for the last half of the afternoon's performance.

Minoru was able to keep his poise until Chōchō sang beneath the cherry blossoms, and the orchestra took up the strains of "Poor Butterfly, 'neath the blossoms waiting, Poor Butterfly!" Minoru felt tears coursing down his cheeks, not for Madame Butterfly but for his own little mother. He furtively wiped them away and refrained from giving his companions a glance.

He had a wild impulse to run home through the snow, to fall upon his bed, to weep and beat his fists in childish frustration. Had his friends known about this and chosen to trap him? Common sense soon cancelled that. This was the only week left before school started again; they had planned the party before they knew what was on the program. So it was none of their doing.

Madame Butterfly sang her farewell song to her young son with such pathos, Minoru could sit still no longer. He rose from his seat without a word, and left. His friends saw him go but thought that he was going to the restroom. They waited for him, but through the remainder of the program they waited in vain. He did not return to his seat.

When all was over for Madame Butterfly and the performance, the lights came on, flooding them with blinding light. The three boys blinked at each other in astonishment. They understood why Minoru had left them so abruptly and were concerned. At a table in the corner of the lobby they talked it over.

"I don't blame him for leaving. I for one, did not think about what it might mean to Minoru. In a vague way, I knew the plot of the thing, but honestly did not connect it with him, and I did not know that it was exactly as it was," Masao was all sympathy.

"I recalled it during the intermission; that is the reason I signalled you, Eiji. I started to suggest that we skip the last half, and go for a walk but it hardly seemed the thing to do in the snow. I wish now that I had suggested something we could have done. *I am* sorry that Minoru had to see it," Toshio told them.

"We all have known from the beginning that Minoru is half-blood, but we have let it make no difference in our friendship for him, have we?" Eiji asked. His friends shook their heads in answer. "He has never intimated that it is a sore point with him, but we could have figured out how he feels by putting ourselves in his place. Of course, he is illegitimate, but Japan is full of those. It seems to be a glaring mistake when there is a mixture of racial strains; yet, it makes the person involved no less worthy; it only makes him stand out like a sore thumb. You don't think that Minoru would do a rash thing, do you?"

"No. He's too sensible for that. He probably went home. Does anyone know where he lives?" Masao asked.

"I do. He pointed out the house to me one day when we were on the train. You can just see the roof of the house across the paddy field," Toshio told them.

"Let's go there now, and let him know that we think nothing amiss."

"It might make him lose face," Masao said, concern for his friend written plainly on his own face. "But the only way to judge these things is to put oneself in the same predicament and think from there. Were I in his place, I'd want my friends to come to me. Let's go."

In half an hour, the three stood puffing from the fast walk from the theater through the still falling snow. They found Minoru's house by the back fence. They pushed their way through the garden shrubs to the front entrance, and rang the bell.

Obasan slid open the door bowed in greeting, and waited for them to state their business. They were strangers to her.

"We are Minoru's friends," Toshio told her. "We'd like to see him for a minute if he is at home."

"He is at home," she told them. "He went to his room saying that he was not feeling well, and would go to bed for a while. Let me go up to ask if he'd like to see you. Just step in out of the cold, please."

The three men stepped into the entrance and closed the outside door against the cold. In a minute she was back.

"The young master says that he will see you on Monday. He feels that he may be taking a cold and he'd not like to expose you to it. He thanks you for coming and sends his regards. Please excuse his rudeness, but he thinks it better for you that you don't come to his room."

They bowed themselves out of the door, and turned down the alley toward town.

"At least we know that he is at home — that is good — I could not have been easy about him if we had not checked." Toshio said, then added, "Wonder who lives there with him? Has either of you ever heard him say?"

No one knew. They went their separate ways; each to his home, after promising to meet on Monday to begin the daily round of school together in the New Year.

Minoru had not gone to bed as he had told Obasan. Instead he had gone to his desk to make notes to himself in his black notebook. Only one notation had he made on this afternoon when he came home with emotions torn to shreds.

Get even with David McLean if it is the last thing you ever do. This Lt. Pinkerton will not get by so easily. My mother did not commit hara-kiri but she did die of a broken heart. My thoughts will continue to work on this thing. He will not escape.

His eyes were red with weeping when Obasan had come to bring the message from his friends. *They cared enough to come.* The thought was warming to him. They were true friends and they would stick by him.

Obasan was very solicitous when she brought up his supper. He had but given an excuse to his friends she knew. She also knew that he had not spoken the true reason for his depression. It was not her business to question; it was her part to see that a good supper should be prepared to lift his troubled spirits.

When Minoru looked at the tray she brought him, he knew that this old woman was wise to his act. Everything that he liked best was on the tray for his enjoyment. One could not resist Obasan's food. Minoru did not try on this lonely, cold night.

After his hearty repast, his spirits lifted; his anger dissipated — vanished into thin air. Only the jottings in the notebook were there to remind him of the earthshaking happenings of that day. He took the notebook and made an outline of his future plans:

1. Let nothing interfere with my medical education.
2. Do everything possible to get to the U.S.A. for study.
3. Locate David M. McLean if possible before going to U.S.A.

He snapped the book closed and shoved it back into the drawer of his desk.

There will be plenty of time for planning ways and means of getting even. Only one thing is sure, if the man is still living, he will pay!

7

On Monday morning when the four friends met at the railway station for their trip to college, Minoru noticed nothing different in their attitudes toward him. He solemnly thanked them for their visit and asked that they come again.

It was not until March that he gave them a special invitation to have dinner with him in his home. Obasan was delighted when he told her that they had accepted his invitation.

The appointed day arrived and began with busy activity on her part. She wanted Minoru's friends to think well of all that went on in his home. She was up early sweeping the walks, flicking from the shoji every speck of dust. Minoru heard the flip-flip-flip of her silk duster before he got up. He smiled to think of her evident pleasure in the preparations she was making.

The purpose for the meeting was to lay final plans for the trip the four friends were making during the cherry-blossom season. Toshio had been appointed to make all preparations for it: reservations on trains and the Japanese Inns. He was to make his report that day.

Minoru had done very little traveling about Japan. Though school trips are definitely a part of every child's education, in his school days, Ojiisan had always some excuse for keeping him at home when his schoolmates went on tour. Minoru knew now that his grandfather had been trying to protect him from the curious, staring populace.

While Obasan went into flurried preparations to receive his guests, Minoru stood looking about his house, trying to see it through the eyes of his friends. This was a traditional Japanese house, plain and unpretentious. He planned to keep his friends in this part of the house; his room upstairs would continue to be his private sanctuary.

He looked at the firebox with its red coals graying about the edges, giving out just enough heat to provide comfort against the chill, lingering in the Spring air. The bit of warmth made the gloomy rooms seem more cheerful.

While he and his guests were seated on zabutons about the hibachi, enjoying the food which Obasan had spent days in preparing for them, the front door bells jangled with special insistence. Minoru heard Obasan leave the kitchen to answer it. She came immediately to whisper the name of the caller to the young master. The guests noticed her nervousness when she spoke to Minoru.

"What in the world can he want?" Minoru asked impatiently.

"It is as I once told you," she said between her teeth. "There is always a fox; he even reminds me of one." She turned again to the kitchen.

Minoru rose from his zabuton and went to the door. A short, pudgy man rubbing his hands together in a washing motion, dressed in a silk haori which had seen its best days, stood before him.

When Minoru bowed to him in greeting, the man reached to take his hand and to pump it up and down as if forcing water from a pump.

"A-a-a, Minoru — now you have become a man! The last time I saw you, you were not a year old — that was when your mother took you from me and returned home to her father. To think, all of this time has gone by and the boy who bears my name, has become a man. I decided that I'd come to see you for myself since your grandfather went and left you all alone."

Minoru stood looking at Mr. Tada, scrutinizing him from head to toe. He knew that his friends were hearing every word; there was no help for that. There was no way to shut up this garrulous little man. His face gave to Minoru the impression that it was fashioned from pliable tan clay into which bits of coals had been punched for eyes.

As he continued to talk, he kept peering around Minoru for a better look at his companions seated in the room. He inhaled hungrily the smell of food issuing from the kitchen; there was definitely a look of hunger about him.

There seemed nothing for Minoru to do but to ask him into the house. It was his intention to seat him in another room and have Obasan serve a tray to him there. But, before Minoru could point the way, Mr. Tada sidled past him and into the room with guests, and was seating himself among them.

"These are my college friends," Minoru told him, giving each of their names in turn.

When Minoru went to the kitchen to tell Obasan to bring an extra tray, he could hear the officious little man still talking to his guests.

"Minoru is my son, at least he bears my name. It has been a long time since I saw him. Now I come to find him a handsome young man." He sucked in his breath over finding these young men to whom he could confide. It would definitely strengthen his purpose of blackmail which he had come to perpetrate. Minoru might lose face to refuse before such a group of his friends. He envisioned himself with the desired sum of money in his pockets, setting off to enjoy the cherry season as befitted one whose relative had been left a wealthy man.

Minoru knew well why this man had come. Suddenly his appetite fled from him but he continued to pick at his food without actually eating. Not so the hungry guest, he not only ate heartily but noisily as well. The three guests looked at him with mirth submerged but shining from their eyes. They kept up a continual chatter among themselves to gloss over the embarrassing situation for their host.

When the meal was over, Minoru excused himself and led his guest upstairs. Mr. Tada stepped into the room and looked about him at the attractive comfort of the place. Minoru heard a sudden in-take of breath as he sank into the chair which Minoru indicated for him. Minoru seated himself opposite him and waited for the intruder to state his business. The man was still enjoying the delicious meal in retrospect, noisily picking and sucking his teeth.

Minoru sat waiting. It was as if Mr. Tada were marshalling all his mental tricks to be played up on this young man before him — this boy who had been left so well off in the world, while his own personal affairs had sunk to a low ebb.

"News of your grandfather's death reached me some time ago but it seemed that it was impossible for me to get here sooner," he lied. "Now that it is holiday time, I managed to get away to come to you."

"What is your business now, Mr. Tada?" Minoru asked knowing that he was knocking him completely off guard.

"At the present, it is not much. The fruit shop which I ran, failed, and other things that I have tried have done little better. Always hard luck overtakes me. Things are hard just now. My wife died some years ago, as you may have heard, and my two children are now apprenticed to relatives."

"I know nothing about your family or about you, Mr. Tada," Minoru said.

"Sō desuka? It is my fault. I should have kept in touch with you — to whom I gave my name. I thought that if you actually knew how things are with me, you might be glad to help tide me over this hard place in my life. I am no longer a young man as you can see for yourself, Minoru."

Minoru could see that and more. There was the high colored floridity seen in the faces of those who continually drink, the excess of which seemed to have drained into bags beneath his eyes, giving him the soulful look of a hound dog. Looking at him sitting in a miserable heap, Minoru was filled with contempt. To this man, his grandfather in his anger and frustration, had literally sold his mother. Minoru's hate for this miserable clod, and for David McLean, flamed so intensely at that moment, he would not have been surprised to see smoke issuing from his nostrils. He was so warm in his person, he seemed to feel heat emitting from his body.

"I wonder if the large amount left to you by your grandfather, my once father-in-law, would make it possible for you to let me have a nominal amount, say 36,000 yen?" Mr. Tada dropped his eyes and waited patiently for an answer.

Minoru continued to look at the despicable man in silence; the man began to squirm as if the chair upon which he sat had become suddenly heated.

"Your grandfather *did* leave you as his sole heir, did he not?" the man asked, letting his eye rove over the well appointed room.

"As a matter of fact, he did, Mr. Tada. He left me well off indeed, but this has nothing to do with you. You have no claim upon my grandfather. I understand that you were well-paid for the thing you did in the nasty situation at the time that I was born."

"You know about it then, do you?" Mr. Tada let his small pig-eyes completely disappear for a moment behind the puffy bags of flesh.

"Yes, everything was explained to me by my grandfather. I have the facts straight; there are no grounds for you to try blackmail. I'm not so young nor so simple as you may think, Mr. Tada."

"It is, after all, my name which you bear." This the man said with a snarl of contempt.

"Would it help you if I gave the name back to you?" Minoru asked. "I have been considering doing it and it would be possible. Not one yen which belongs to me will ever come into your hands, Mr. Tada, if I can help it, and, there is nothing that you can do about it." Minoru had never heard his own voice so hard or determined.

Mr. Tada was wise enough to know when he was defeated in his purpose. Pretense fell from him like a sudden letting go of a cape about his shoulders. "I don't know what the law would say about this, Minoru, but I should think that you would feel that you could spare this little from your plenty."

"There will be no sharing with you, Mr. Tada. I want no dealings with you — just as you wanted no more dealings with my mother and me when I happened to be born with the look of the West in my face. I should think that this same pride would have forbidden your coming here to beg from me."

This was touché. The little man knew it. He rose to go, shoulders drooping, as if someone had suddenly removed the stopper from the toe of a rubber doll. Still in the act of wash-rubbing his hands, he was let out the door to go his shiftless way.

Minoru turned back to his friends who paused in their conversation as he entered. Suddenly he wanted them to know the truth about himself and about the man's visit. He found himself telling them of his youthful bafflement and shame. He read to them Ojiisan's letter but he did not show the picture of his parents nor reveal the fact that he might someday be able to trace him.

They listened in silence but he could feel their sympathy enfold him like a cloak. When he had finished, Toshio spoke, "Minoru, it would be false to let you think that we knew nothing of this. Anyone looking at you knows that you are Eurasian without having to be told. I could never blame anyone for a thing over which he no control. That would be as senseless as blaming a deformed person for his affliction."

"That's exactly the way I feel," Masao said. "It could be, Minoru, that you are more fortunate than you think. In this new age of Japan, when Western ways flow freely into Japan, mixed blood could be an asset. Your American blood has given you a few things which we could envy: your height, your more than average good looks, and already, though your American blood has nothing to do with it — you possess your own home."

Minoru smiled wanly as Masao was talking. He was warmed by his friends' attitude.

"You can count yourself fortunate to have some money in your own name. You must have discovered by now that few barriers will not give way before money's pressure." Eiji said this with a knowing look.

"Thank you all. It is a relief that I have at last brought myself to speak of this to you. It has all been very heavy for me since I was old enough to know that I am different. Now that you know it, I do not feel so heavy." Minoru unconsciously placed his hand against his chest.

Minoru asked them about the wisdom of changing his name to Takahashi. The advantages and disadvantages were batted back and forth with the final decision for him to continue to carry the name he was known by in the town. "After all," Toshio said, "what does one's name actually matter save for the content that we personally put into it?"

Toshio was ready to make his report, so all else was put aside for the moment. Before the close of the college, they had made tentative plans for all the places they wished most to visit. Eiji's choice had been a tour of Takamatsu, the jewel of a city across the Inland Sea from Kobe. Masao had spoken in favor of a visit to Ise Shrine. "Every Japanese is supposed to go there sometime in his life and I have never been."

Minoru had never visited the national shrine, but his first choice was Hiroshima. "I want to see that spot. Ojiisan would never hear to my going; he wouldn't even talk about it or the bomb which destroyed it."

"Well, since we are to take a swing around the Inland Sea by way of Ise Shrine, let's visit Oshima — the Pearl Island while we are near. When I was very small I went there with the family. It was a highlight of my childhood. It may prove uninteresting to me now but I'd like to see it again," Masao said.

With these places in mind, Toshio had worked out the itinerary.

"The trip as it is planned now," explained Toshio, "will start by going first to Ise-that part by train. From there by bus we'll go to Oshima and there we'll spend our first night. The next day we'll take a boat around the Inland Sea to Takamatsu, ending our swing at Hiroshima, then home by train."

"It's going to be fun traveling about, but let's travel light with only our knapsacks. Too much baggage is a jama (bother) when all trains are so crowded."

"If the days remain fair, the cherry blossoms will be at their height when we start. Let's hope the rains hold off," Eiji said.

After his friends had gone, Minoru sat thinking over all that had transpired: it had been his friends' first visit to his home, the first time he had seen the man whose name he falsely bore, and they had planned his first trip in cherry-blossom time.

He sat remembering his conversation with the pudgy, cringing Mr. Tada, and wondered what his mother's life had been with such a man.

The idea of his coming here to blackmail me into giving him money. I'd like to choke him with my bare hands! These thoughts made him feel so violent he deliberately transferred his thoughts to the trip which was to begin on Monday. He was like a child in his keen anticipation of a vacation with his friends. For them it would be repeating things they had done before; for Minoru it would be a thrilling first.

He went up to his room and began to assort things which would fit into his brand new knapsack, the first he had ever possessed.

ON THE TRAIN TO ISE, the four boys began to reach back in their memories for all they could remember about the ancient spot, and to recall reasons why every Japanese is supposed to visit the place before he dies.

"It has something to do with the country's beginning," Masao said, "but what, I do not know!"

"Don't look at me for the answer," Toshio was laughing at his ignorance. "Maybe Minoru knows. Do you, Minoru?"

"More than the rest of you, evidently," he replied in mock superiority. "You know, don't you, about the god, Izanagi, and the goddess, Izanami?" This he said in tones calculated to shame them for their ignorance.

When they shook their heads in answer, Minoru asked again, "Where have you been all your lives not to know these things?"

"We all started to school during the time of the American Army of occupation, remember, and these legends which had been used to solidify the nation for the great holocaust, had been pushed back where they belong — as legends — nothing more. The Emperor himself exploded the theory that we Japanese are a god-race. That much I do know," Toshio admitted.

"Minoru," Eiji said, "you are a continual puzzle to me. You are the one of us who is not fully Japanese, yet you know more folklore than all of us put together."

"Yes, and remember, I had Ojiisan, who was Old Japan and never let me forget it for a minute. Japan was conquered, but Ojiisan never was! The old man's one ambition was to tip the scale of my life to the Japanese side of me. He continually stuffed me with things Japanese, both fact and fiction."

"Go on. Tell us the story so that it will be fresh in our minds when we arrive at Ise," Masao begged.

"Well, from the couple of heavenly beings, Izanagi and Izanami, who were encircling the watery globe, flying in and out of the low-lying clouds, Izanagi let a few drops of moisture dribble from his trident into the oceans. Presto — the Japanese Kingdom came into being."

"How about the rest of the earth?" Masao asked with a devilish tilt in his words.

"Oh, they were formed from the flotsom-jetsam which adhered and floated above the world's oceans. That's how!"

The boys laughed uproariously at Minoru's serious mien. Undaunted he continued, "Poor Izanami was burned to a crisp when she gave birth to Fire, but her spouse would not give up, he went on procreating like an oyster: Amaterasu, the sun goddess sprang from his left eye, Tsukinokami — the moon god — sprang from his right eye; Susanoo — the sword god — sprang from his nostrils."

"So much for the gods. How about the humans?" Masao was leading him on.

"Susanoo, the old dog, ravished his sister, Amaterasu, who immediately hid in a cave taking with her the light of the sun. The two brother gods, acted as if another princess had come to make sport with them before the cave in the moon's light. Amaterasu, hearing this merry-making, came out of hiding, bringing back the light of the world with her.

"In time a male offspring was born to her. He, in turn, produced Jimmu — our first Emperor — our founding father. He is said to have come to the throne in 660 B.C. Now my story is told!"

"I can take it from there," Eiji volunteered. "From that time the Imperial line has remained unbroken down to our day, some 2656 years ago, that is, if we choose to close our historical eyes to the fact that many of our Emperors have been offspring of concubines, who in no way were related to this imperial line of Japan. It just makes a better story this way and sounds better."

"What I'd like someone to explain to me," Toshio said, "is how before the war the Military took these old absurdities from the national closet and dusted them off to make them believable for the Japanese populace. They *somehow* made the people believe them as truth, for they immediately began acting as though they actually were god-people with the god-given right to rule the world. Someday I hope some historian will get to work and give us the truth about it."

"If ever such a book is written, I'm afraid some foreigner will have to write it, possibly in English. Japanese people will not talk about this period, at least, my professors of history won't, though they must remember it."

"They want it to slip into obscurity, possibly because they are ashamed to admit that it happened. But, some day the truth will be known; someone will ferret out the facts and record them. Did your grandfather talk to you about this, Minoru?" Eiji asked.

"About the war years, Grandfather said very little, though I have often heard him say that the Japanese people were grossly misled by the Military. He found those years too bitter and baffling to be discussed with anyone."

They left the train at the station and began to wander about the great park surrounding the National Shrine. Thousands of others had chosen this day to visit the shrine, not so much to worship, as to see the blossoms and to have a break from their monotonous lives.

On the train trip down to Ise, they had passed village after village where the cherry blossoms stood row upon row along the street, frantic in their blooming, foaming a pink froth of blossoms until the very air about them seemed to reflect the rosy glow. Here at Ise it was the same; through the ancient cryptomerias, close-wrapped in their ancient memories, one could here and there glimpse a rash of pink blossoms softening the otherwise stark vista of the giant trunks.

The boys were silent as they walked beneath the trees which had witnessed the happenings of centuries. Minoru felt, as he passed beneath them in well-defined paths, that he had stepped back through the doors of antiquity. The Japanese part of him responded to the dim past's call; he felt a spiritual impact of the fixed faith of millions who tenaciously held to these old legends, fearful lest their hearts be void without them.

In their room at the Inn that night, Toshio spoke of his reaction to the afternoon's experiences. "It was almost like stepping into a fairy tale in my imagination. I seemed to have left behind the modern world with all of its scientific knowledge, its electricity, radios, televisions. I liked the feeling for a little while but it is good to be back in the world to which I belong."

At Oshima — Pearl Island — they watched the young, thinly clad women diving in the chilly water to bring to the surface the one-year-old oysters which would be injected with the grain of shell, around which the pearls would form, and, felt as if they were seeing again the film strips which every school child sees over and over.

The glowing spring day was perfect for their motor launch ride about the bay. They stretched themselves upon the deck benches to watch the receding shore line, the passing pearl farms, the clumps of women knifing the pearls from the slimy oysters.

Minoru lay flat on his back, looking only at the inverted blue bowl of heaven, fascinated by the puffs of clouds which seemed to be sailing with them. He wondered how long this feeling of absolute peace and well-being could be sustained: devoid of all passion of anger, of hate against those who had put snarls into his life. He devoutly wished that it were possible to hold the peace which now was his, as he lay in the warm sunshine with the chilly winds playing over his face. Even here, the habitual fretful thoughts, which often plagued his mind, tried to intrude themselves upon his thoughts; he willfully resisted them. Nothing was going to steal these moments from him; he might never again have another such soul-satisfying experience.

During the traveling days, Minoru was to experience many such days. He loved them all; the beauty of Takamatsu was almost over-powering in its perfection. Minoru felt that he would like to evade his companions and, like a rabbit, hide in the beautiful park to watch the populace pass in review. He stood so long upon the curved bridge, his companions called to him to hurry before he was lost in the throng.

Not one of the boys had counted on such an emotional impact from his visit to Hiroshima. When they left the streetcar, which stopped in front of the great Memorial Park, newly built over the spot where hell fell from the sky on that August morning in 1945, they walked to a vantage spot to look over the landscape.

"If one were ignorant of all that took place here on August sixth, thirteen years ago, this would be just a meticulously landscaped Park stretching over this plain," Eiji said more to himself than to his friends.

"With that skeleton building over there one would be sure to ask questions. It was left there on purpose to remind everyone of what happened in a twinkling of an eye; a sturdy concrete and steel building was reduced to a scab on the horizon. It gives one the shakes to look at it," Masao said.

Each year, on the fateful anniversary of the dropping of the bomb, T.V.s and radios blared forth the awful details of the tragedy so that no Japanese could possibly forget them. They stood noticing how Nature had done her best to hide man's wrathful acts, but the skeleton building, gaping at them from a distance, was untouched by Nature's camouflage.

They turned to go up the steps to the Museum containing relics of that fateful morning, and filed slowly past the glass cases holding tragic reminders of that loosed power: big brass urns melted into weird puddles of metal, huge jars congealed into globs of glass, garments, which had on that day clothed human bodies, hung limp and scorched without a torn seam yet the solid flesh had vanished — evaporated! Minoru turned with tears flooding his eyes to watch the faces of those who were marching past these horrors. Each face was set in tragic mold. He felt the tears of pity for all mankind coursing down his cheeks. When he stood to one side to surreptitiously wipe them away, he found himself beside an American woman who wept softly into her handkerchief.

As they were leaving the place, Toshio pointed to a yellow handbill framed under glass.

"I've always heard that the Americans dropped handbills to warn the populace of what they were about to loose upon the city, and I've heard it refuted. Here we see it, so it is true. This tells them to flee to the mountains. I wonder why they did not flee?"

No one answered until they were outside the building with the fresh spring winds blowing across their faces.

"Would you have believed it?" Minoru asked. "For five years they were fed with constant propaganda. *That* warning must have seemed more of the same to them."

Before leaving the park they walked to stand beside the memorial stone where the thousands of names of those who were known to have perished were entombed. While they stood before it, a woman, with an armful of fresh flowers, came to place them before the stone. She stood for a moment in resigned silence, then turned sorrowfully away. The boys did the same.

Nothing more was said about the bomb until they were back at their inn, and dinner had been served them there. They had been emotionally torn by their day abroad in the newly-rebuilt city of Hiroshima, but the food, the soaking hot baths did much to revive them. Lying prone about the straw mat floor, clad in the clean kimonas furnished by the inn, they began again to discuss their reactions to the things both seen and experienced.

"I found it very hard not to hate Americans when we walked through the museum. I realize that it is American money which has rebuilt this city and especially Memorial Park, but that can never wipe out the hard fact that it was *their* bomb dropped, knowing that thousands of innocent people would lose their lives," Eiji spoke with bitterness.

"I suppose all of us had something of the same feeling, Eiji, but let's not forget that the Americans did warn the people. Let's give them credit." As he spoke Minoru was keenly aware that it was his father's country which had destroyed the city.

"Let's not forget, too, that we Japanese started the war against America," Toshio, the historian, said, "I, for one, do not believe that America would have entered the war had Japan not bombed Pearl Harbor."

"Ojiisan thought that too, Toshio. I've often heard him say so to neighbors who talked of the dastardly attack on Hiroshima. He always reminded them of the sneak attack on Pearl Harbor; he also reminded them how many of our men were saved from the suicide squads who were ready in case of invasions. He would say, 'Were our boys who were forced to fight this war any more guilty than those who perished by the bomb? Is it actually worse to kill children in school than soldiers? Who *is* guilty in time of war? Do the innocent ever escape or the guilty pay for their folly?"

Such talk went on among them until late that night. It was Masao who asked the last question which made them grow quiet in deep thought.

"If we Japanese had had the bomb at that desperate time, would we not have used it against our enemy? I know that we *would* have. There is nothing good about war. Anyone who fights a war, fights to win or they are stupid. It is the ones who provoke the wars that are guilty criminals."

"Right, Masao, we were duped by our Military war mongers. It's a bit early to judge whether we were trapped against our wills or whether most Japanese liked the idea. I'm glad I was too small to know or to go. Never do I want war to come to earth again. Surely there must be some better way. Hate is a dreadful thing; it scorches most severely those who harbor it within themselves."

Minoru went to sleep thinking about Toshio's words. Deep in his heart he was harboring a burning hatred for David McLean. It burned in him in the stillness of the night when his thoughts grew dark and baffling. If he kept this hate, would it someday scorch him?

The picture of the American and his young mother, standing beneath the cherry trees years ago, made him writhe in agony in the lilac darkness of the inn room, while his companions peacefully slept.

MONTHS AFTER HIS TRIP, Minoru woke to a white world. Through the glass panels of the doors, he could see the snow like fluffy down upon the dwarfed trees in the garden. The little electric stove which he had turned on earlier made the room comfortable, almost too comfortable, as he lay considering the long cold day away from home.

This was his last year of college; Minoru found the fact hard to believe, yet, he was glad to think that college work was almost behind him. He had become so immersed in his studies, life now held very little else for him. Sometimes he longed for the days when it had been possible to have more contact with his friends. It saddened him to think of how life literally turns one into new channels, leaving the old ones neglected. He tried to remember how long it had been since he had seen his old friends.

Masao, he knew, had left college to enter the Language University in Kobe; he aspired to be a teacher of Romance Languages. The last time Minoru had bumped into Masao on a crowded train, they had had only a few minutes in which to catch up with each other. Masao had been full of new thoughts, which seemed to be pulling him into new channels. From what Minoru was able to understand, he judged the new ideas to be communistic. This philosophy, so rampant among students during the prewar days, had often been discussed with him by Ojiisan who had feared what it might do to the Japanese Nation, especially since it had sprung to life in Russia, Japan's enemy. Sparks of it seemed to have lasted out the war, and were now bursting into flames in New Japan. Here and there Minoru had felt the heat of it, but this was the first time he had detected a flame. After that chance meeting, repeatedly, Masao called him on the telephone to invite him to some of the meetings.

"Please come, Minoru. You will find a bunch of fellows — girls too — who have the same ideas about things as you have, the same ambitions, the same aims. You will like what you hear, I'm sure." *How does Masao know what ambitions, aims and ideas I have? He might be surprised if I ever revealed them to him. I am sure I will not like his bunch nor anything they stand for.*

There were definitely times when he longed for a group with whom he could identify, but he knew something of the communistic aims in the world, and was against them all, so he never responded to Masao's invitations.

It was almost as if the thinking of the things in early morning had brought it about — for that day, above the heads of the pushing, shoving throngs on the trains, he saw Toshio. They waved to each other, and began to worm their ways to a meeting spot in the center of the car. Before they could reach it, the crowd had flowed into it and they were stopped in their tracks.

In sign language they agreed to meet on the bus. Minoru had never seen Toshio look so well. He studied his face, and realized how much he had missed this friend whose mind never ceased its search for truth.

On the crowded bus it was impossible for them to do more than greet each other and exchange a few words as they swung on the straps.

Before they parted company at the college gate, hurrying to classes in opposite directions, they made a date to meet that afternoon for dinner in a Kobe restaurant.

At the appointed time and place at Nishinomiya station, they met for the short ride into Kobe. They found a quiet spot in a restaurant on Motomachi, and there began to pick up the threads of their lives which had led them off in different directions.

"I saw Masao not too long ago," Minoru told Toshio. "He is studying at the Language University. From what he told me, I judge that he has fallen into a communistic group there. He is certainly filled with enthusiasm for it all. He's invited me to the meetings but I want nothing to do with that group."

"I don't see why anyone would want what communists peddle. How could anyone in present day Japan want them? We have but to ask ourselves, 'What brought Japan back from the brink of financial collapse?' The answer, 'Capitalist money.' Even a blind person can see that our rise from the ashes of defeat has been nothing short of miraculous, new in the world's history. I hope someday the historians will tell of our rise and the reasons for it for future generations and the whole world to read."

Minoru smiled and said, "How about writing it yourself, Toshio? You are living through it; you're a child of Japan's affluent age."

"It's a thought," Toshio shyly admitted, pleased by the compliment.

"When have you seen Eiji? What is he doing with himself?" Minoru asked.

"I see him occasionally. He has found a new channel-interest too, in the new religion, Soka Gakkai. Do you know anything about it, Minoru?"

"Yes, a little," Minoru acknowledged, "only what I've read, that it is having phenomenal growth in Japan. "Eiji has joined them?" he asked.

"I think so, but with his heavy work schedule, he's not able to give much time to it but he really thinks that it is to be the new way for Japan's youth."

"What do you think, Toshio?"

"It seems that it has much to offer in many directions: ready-made friends, a guarantee to business success and getting ahead in the world. It is a mixture of Communism, Buddhism and Christianity; more materialistic than anything else. Materialism seems to be the theme of this age; it's a shame, but it is true."

"It all seems so different from Old Japan. My grandfather said that there would be many changes and only Time would tell us which would be a blessing, which a curse. I don't know enough about Soka Gakkai to have an opinion about it," Minoru admitted.

"I don't either, but from what Eiji has told me, I feel that there are underlying threats to our country. It is not just a religious philosophy, it has dangerous underlying currents of political implications. No one thought that Fascism was a threat to Germany and the world when it first began. But before the Germans realized it, the thing had them in its clutches. Soka Gakkai will bear watching in Japan."

"Such devious ways we are taking, Toshio. This accounts for Eiji and Masao, how about us? I can speak for myself. With all the science courses which are to lead me into medicine, I simply bone away, trying to keep my head above water. I have become a sponge — taking it all in, working toward my goal."

"What is your goal, Minoru?"

"To get college behind me and the medical course which follows, then get to America for at least one year of graduate study in the specialty which I shall choose when I know more things."

As Minoru spoke the words, he knew that his goal was not entirely that of graduate study. He had another matter in mind. It was a consuming fire in his vitals day and night.

"How about your English?" Toshio asked.

"I'm weak in it. I know that I should be more proficient but German is more important for me now. So many of our medical texts are in the German. We *must,* as medical students, be able to understand as we read. I wish I had Masao's love for languages."

"What professor do you have for English this year, Minoru?"

"Dr. Brace. He is fine; it's just that I am a poor student. We are fortunate in having so many Americans on the faculty. At least we learn the *tune* of the language. That will be a help when I finally go to America.

"How about *your* English, Toshio?"

"I am very poor in it too and am ashamed. So many of our history books are in English; I must improve. When I asked my professor to suggest a teacher to help me, he recommended one of the American wives as a private tutor. I have been studying with her now for six months."

Minoru laughed aloud. "An American woman! I'd be scared to death of one. Is she a good teacher?"

"She is not just good, she is excellent — the best I've had. I felt as you do about it at first. She seemed so different from a Japanese woman: so straight forward, so frank in her approach to things. But Mrs. Grady put me at ease immediately, and before I knew what was taking place, she had me talking to her in English. She was working out her own methods; they are working for me. I am not in the least nervous with her. We chat along now like two old friends."

Minoru saw the smile of genuine pleasure flit across his friend's face.

"Mrs. Grady is a Christian and she is teaching me as we go along. At first I resented it, but she told me plainly that she would teach no one with whom she could not speak of her faith. The way she put it made it seem logical and right to me, so I gave in. She said to me, 'No one can understand the English language, English literature, Western Music or Art without knowing what Christianity teaches. Our way of life, our culture, our thinking all have their roots in Christian teachings. These have formed us into the people that we have become."

"Since I have been with her, I have become interested in her philosophy which stems, of course, from the teaching of Jesus Christ."

Minoru sat still, unspeaking.

"Someday I'd like to take you with me to one of her Bible classes on Sunday afternoons."

Minoru switched the conversation to other things. *First Communism — then Soka Gakkai — now Christianity! Where will I turn?*

In December Toshio wrote a note inviting Minoru to a special Christmas meeting of the Bible Class to be held in Mrs. Grady's home. His first impulse was to refuse the invitation, but the loneliness of the season with only Obasan to keep him company, made him accept it. He telephoned Toshio to say that he would meet him at the appointed place.

When they arrived at the large yellow stucco house and stood waiting to enter, Minoru let his eyes rove over the wide expanse of it, realizing that this was the first experience in a foreign house. Mrs. Grady answered their ring and welcomed them warmly into her home. She shook hands with them and showed them where to leave their coats.

In the long living room with its lighted Christmas tree and an open fire on the hearth, Minoru looked about him at the strangeness. An open fire was a novelty to him, and never had he seen such a brilliantly lighted Christmas tree.

Twenty Japanese boys sat about the great room, showing plainly that they were accustomed to being here and felt at ease. They conversed freely with one another before the program began. The meaning of the word "Christmas" was explained to them by one of the boys in clear and rather fluent English. While Mrs. Grady read to them the second chapter of Luke's gospel, each person who had not brought a Bible had one put into his hands. So clearly and deliberately did she read that Minoru felt for the first time in his life, he was understanding as the words were being read. This was a new experience in understanding which gave him a thrill of hope that someday he would be able both to read English and understand it.

After the program they played games which seemed to be familiar to the other boys. Minoru caught himself laughing with the abandonment of a child at the delightful guessing games. As they sat about the room enjoying the unfamiliar dessert, Minoru watched the faces of the students and saw happiness there.

I might come to feel at home in this group; I might even feel not too strange with Mrs. Grady. As this thought flicked through his mind, he smiled to think of what his grandfather would think of this.

When they left the house that night, Mrs. Grady placed a small package, wrapped in white tissue and tied with red ribbon, into each hand. Minoru slipped this into his pocket, and wondered about all that he had seen and heard as he walked home under the crisp December sky.

Minoru opened his package as soon as he was in his room. When he untied the ribbon, he saw that it was a Bible written in both English and Japanese, he turned to the chapter that had been read by Mrs. Grady in Luke's gospel, and read it in Japanese for a better understanding. He slowly closed the book and thought, *This makes about as much sense as the story of the founding of Japan. For me, a person steeped in science and scientific studies, this would be impossible to believe.*

He stuck the book back into a cubby hole of his desk and left it there, but the things which Mrs. Grady had told them stuck in his mind like a burr. He was impatient with himself for having gone to such a meeting. *The idea that there is a God; one who loved the world so much that He came in the form of a baby to live as a man. Ridiculous!* He tried to brush the whole thing from his mind.

When next Toshio invited him to attend the Bible class, Minoru flatly refused. His grandfather's influence was yet too strong upon him: the teacher was a foreign woman, this was a foreign religion; it was not for him. When he said as much to Toshio, he was surprised by his answer, "That sounds strange coming from you, Minoru. After all, one half of you reaches back into the Western world, and like Mrs. Grady says, you can never understand the English speaking world unless you know what Christianity teaches."

"I'm going to America to study medicine, not American culture," Minoru said more tartly than he intended. As he said the words, his thoughts ran back to a sort of worn track in his mind, *I will go to America to find the man who fathered me and when I do —* his mind never could go further than that. He had no desire to hurt physically, but there were other ways of hurting such as blackmail. With this thought, the pathetic picture of Mr. Tada always came to his mind, and he knew that he'd never stoop to anything so low as that. *There are yet three more years,* he told himself. *In that time I can surely think of some way to get even with David McLean.*

When the time came for plunging into the study of medicine, Minoru was ready for it. Study was his steady companion, and though his friends chided him about sticking too closely to his studies, he never considered that study was work. His grandfather had studied something as long as he lived. In the evenings, when work was over in the garden, and he had taken his walk in the mauve twilight, watching the stars prick through the velvety darkness, he would come silently into the room where Minoru was at work, and without a word, get his own books to study.

Before retiring to his room for the night, Ojiisan would smoke his one pipe of tobacco, a signal for Minoru to discuss anything which seemed uppermost in his mind. He never ceased to be interested in anything which had happened in Minoru's day.

Often on rainy days, even when Minoru was very small, they had vied with one another at brush painting. His grandfather could take a blank sheet of paper, and, in the twinkling of an eye, paint numerous horses cavorting on a hill, or a school of fish streaking across an expanse of water.

This ability to paint was proving valuable in Minoru's medical studies. He could draw the organs of the body to scale and paint them. His fellow students were all anxious to look through his notebooks when it came time for their examinations.

10

ON THE TRAIN, returning from Kyoto one day, Minoru rushed to a vacant place to find that he had seated himself beside a leggy American youth. Without seeming to do so, Minoru looked askance at this tall fellow and decided to risk a bit of English practice on him.

"Excuse me." The young American looked up from the absorbing story he was reading in his magazine, and turned an altogether engaging smile upon this Japanese who had spoken to him.

"Excuse me," Minoru tried again, "but-where-are-you-going?"

"I am going to Takarazuka." Wonder of wonders, the foreigner had understood his question. A surge of pride went through Minoru like a hot drink on a cold day. The American had answered distinctly, then added, "Where are you going?"

"I-too-go-to-Takarazuka. Why-are-you-in-Japan?" Minoru asked, then wondered at his own brashness. The American seemed to take no offense but answered clearly.

"I am here to study the Japanese language and culture; but, to make that possible, I am teaching English at a High School in Takarazuka. Do you live there?"

"Yes, I-live-Takarazuka," Minoru answered haltingly. "Where-is-your-address?"

"I am presently staying at a Japanese Inn close by the school, but I am trying to find a Japanese home that will take me in. I feel that is the best way to learn things Japanese. Do you happen to know of such a place?"

Minoru's mind was so busy working that he merely shook his head in answer.

"I am going to put advertisements in the newspapers. Today, at school, the principal wrote one for me in Japanese. I shall place it also in English newspapers because I'd prefer the family with whom I live to be able to speak some English."

The young man handed the slip of paper to Minoru, who perused it and sat holding it in his hands. There was something so right about the thoughts which were coursing through his mind: *Why can't I ask this young American to come to live at my home? Obasan would not mind, he'd be company for me, he could teach me English and the American way; I could teach him Japanese and Japanese culture. It would be preparation for going to America. But how can I say this to him?*

Before handing back the piece of paper, Minoru turned in his seat to look full into the young American's face. He liked what he saw there: a slim ruddy face beneath a shock of light brown hair, snapping blue eyes which seemed to send out sparks of merriment. His too generous mouth seemed resolutely shut to keep from escaping boisterous laughter which waited a chance for an outlet. Minoru decided to risk speaking his thoughts.

"I have house. You like to live there, I like."

"You mean that your family would let me board with them? What family have you?"

"I have myself and my family servant, Obasan."

"You mean you live alone except for the family servant? No one else is in your home?"

"Yes, that is so. I live by self. When we get Takarazuka, you come my house. See. If you like, I like; we talk."

Minoru could tell that this turn of events was a surprise for the young man. He could almost feel him turning the proposition over in his mind.

"Are you a student?" the American asked.

"Yes, Medical School in Kyoto. Every day I ride train from Takarazuka."

Before the train arrived at the station, many such questions had been batted back and forth between the two young men. Minoru led his new acquaintance through the maze of alleys until they reached the one leading to his home. Suddenly he turned to the American to ask, as if it were his first need to know, "What is your name?"

"I am Joe Harden from Eugene, Oregon," he answered and extended his hand to be shaken. Minoru took it uncertainly, then bowed from the waist.

"I, Minoru Tada."

As they walked shoulder to shoulder up the lane together, each noticed that they were perfectly matched for height. Joe noticed something else; there was a strangeness about this handsome young man. He was not all Japanese, that was plain to see, but in any man's measurement, he was a beautiful specimen of manhood.

Once inside the gate, Joe looked about the carefully cultivated garden.

"Do you keep this garden yourself?"

"No. A medical student has not time for garden — only for study."

Before entering the house, Minoru rang the bell to alert Obasan. Immediately she was there, bowing before the strange, foreign visitor. In Japanese Minoru introduced them. Obasan was immediately on her knees touching her head to the floor in welcome. She led them into the room and bustled away to bring hot tea to her master and his guest.

Joe Harden looked about him in this completely strange setting of Old Japan. Everything about the place was completely foreign to him, yet there was a charm, a restfulness in its stark simplicity, which were soul-satisfying.

When they had finished tea, Minoru took his guest upstairs to his room. Once there, Joe was filled with curiosity. He had known by looking at Minoru that there was a foreign strain in him, and the room bore out his conclusion. He looked about with genuine appreciation. Minoru caught the question in his face, and said quickly.

"After Grandfather left, I decided to fix my room as I like. I like comfort of West. Here I have."

"You certainly do have your comfort. It's a good study room for a student."

Minoru led the way from this room out on the balcony overlooking the river, then into the adjoining room.

"Here you stay, if you like. If you want to live Japanese style, yes. If you want American style, we fix."

In Minoru's room they spent the afternoon discussing arrangements for Joe Harden to become a member of the household. Joe looked upon the arrangement as ideal from his point of view: the two of them could swap languages; by living as a Japanese he would be introduced to a culture not known to him. Minoru's unspoken joy over the arrangement was that he would be preparing for a sojourn in America. He felt like a wise spider busily weaving his web. He could hardly believe his good fortune in having by chance met this young American, and persuaded him to come to live in his home.

Before the week was over, Joe had moved his few belongings into the new quarters and was feeling at home there. He liked Obasan immediately, and he liked the room, changed only by adding a bed, a chest of drawers and a typing table for a desk. Most of all he liked Minoru Tada. There was something intriguing and determined about this young man. He could wait to find out what it was. In the meantime he felt his curiosity putting out feelers in all directions.

Almost eighteen months were to pass before Joe fully understood the mystery which clung to his host. On a raw night, when the winds howled about the house and the ground was being blanketed with a heavy snow, Minoru brought out the bundle of papers received after his grandfather's funeral. During the months which Joe had spent with him, Minoru found himself speaking English almost without thought. Joe, in his spare time, read stories into the tape recorder; these Minoru played over and over until he could recite them by heart. Soon the sentences became his own; the words were his to toss about recklessly in new combinations. Joe reserved the right to correct him at any time; Minoru had the same right with Joe's Japanese. His progress was more rapid than Joe's, since the American had to start at the beginning.

On this blustery night after they had finished their "swap of tongues" — as Joe termed their sessions — he suddenly had the desire to take this friend into his confidence and share his constant heartache as he had never shared it with anyone before.

Holding the packet of letters in his hands, he told Joe his life's story from the beginning. He translated Ojiisan's letter into English and showed him the picture of the couple — his parents — beneath the blooming cherry trees.

Without comment Joe listened quietly to Minoru's recital, felt the strain of anger and frustration underlying all that he said. As he looked at the photograph of the American who had fathered this son, his sympathies were all with his friend who had suffered throughout his life because of the accident of his birth. Joe was too young and too inexperienced to know how to show his sympathy. He had a definite feeling that life often played some very queer tricks or that men played queerer tricks with life. He could not have put this thought into words, for they were brand new ones for him.

Joe sat vainly trying for words which might ease Minoru's pain, written in his deep, dark eyes.

"You've never seen your father?" he asked for the want of something better to say.

"No, never, but some day I will see him if I can track — what do you say in English?"

" 'Trace him,' is the expression you want," Joe told him. "That should be possible since we know the city he is from, and we know that he is a doctor. The American Medical Association will have some record of him, surely. We can locate him all right. I'll help you."

Minoru's heart beat high with hope. It was for this that the idea of inviting the American to share his home had forced him to issue the invitation. It was for this that he had waited and trained himself. It was for this that all of his past energies had been directed and expended. He was breathing hard now that hope of actual accomplishment was at hand.

"Joe, would you take this task? Write letters — anything to find David McLean? I shall see him when I get to America someday. I want to meet him face to face."

Joe noticed the trembling of his friend's hands, the intensity in his voice, and wondered. He noted also the labored breathing and the extreme brightness of his eyes.

"Why do you want this so much, Minoru? Do you want to reveal yourself to a man who does not know that you exist?" Joe gave a sudden jarring laugh, "Boy, that would really be something, for a full grown son to appear out of the nowhere and say, 'Here I am, Doctor — I am your son!' "

Though Joe laughed at this, Minoru was not able to follow these quick-spoken words enough to get the full meaning. He kept his unsmiling composure and simply stated again his desire to trace Dr. David McLean.

"Will you start at once, Joe?" Minoru asked solemnly.

"If you say so, Minoru. It might be fun to face him with yourself, then again it might be something of a shock for him. You're a fine hunk of manhood, Minoru. He might even be overjoyed to see you. On the other hand, it might play havoc with his life as it now is lived. But, if you want me to trace him, I'll start tonight. Give me pen and paper. There's no time like the present."

Minoru had him sit at the desk and gave him pen and paper. The first letter of inquiry was sent to the American Medical Association, Washington, D.C.

Letters flew back and forth across the Pacific. Joe Harden was vitally interested in the thing now, and since he was returning to the States in June, he wanted to have it sewed up before he left.

On a day in spring, when the world was a riot of blooming, the long-desired letter came. It was waiting for Joe when he got to the house. Minoru, who had returned first, handled the letter, turning it over and over in his hands, sensing that his search was at an end. His emotions were mixed: with part of himself he wished that he had deliberately forgotten this despised man, for life as it now stood was proving intensely interesting for him; with the other part he wanted nothing more than to have the man in his grasp — at least to know for a certainty where he could be found. He often dreamed of the encounter with this strange man and the pain he would inflict upon him.

When Joe entered the door, Minoru handed him the letter without comment; sat in controlled silence while his friend tore open the envelope and read it in silence, then handed it to Minoru. Before Minoru could read it, he said, "We've tracked him to his lair, Minoru. Dr. David M. McLean, by this account is quite a boy! Chief of Surgeons at one of the great medical centers of our country. You might begin by throwing out the chest with pride that you were sired by such a winner. He really is somebody — Chief of Surgeons! Boy — now that's one for the books!"

Minoru began to read the letter for himself. A lump of unshed tears rose in his throat, turmoil was in his mind. Nothing of what he was thinking did he attempt to share with the American. He kept his reactions close-locked in his heart. He did remember to express his thanks to Joe for all the trouble he had gone to to find the man. Then he folded the letter carefully and put it in the canvas bag with his other precious documents. These he returned to the locked drawer of his desk and kept all of his resolutions strictly to himself.

11

MINORU PAUSED to take stock of himself and his chosen profession and began to wonder if he were emotionally equipped for the study of medicine and all that it involved. It began when, in the study of anatomy, he went for the first time into the dissecting laboratory and saw his first cadaver. He found himself almost in a state of shock as he stood there. There was something appalling about a human body after life has left it, stark and stiff — and empty. He found himself trembling with fear.

During those next days he found it difficult to swallow his food; sleep did not come easily to him and there were troubled dreams. Each day he was thankful for Joe's presence when he arrived home at evening. Joe noticed the change in Minoru: the flagging appetite, and the pallor which seemed to encircle his mouth and draw the flesh a bit tautly over his nose.

"Minoru," Joe asked one night when Obasan had removed his almost untouched tray with a loud cluck of disapproval, "what's eating you?" Seeing the puzzled look on Minoru's face, Joe changed the wording of the question, "What's the matter with you lately? You are not like yourself and you don't look well!"

"Nothing. Why?" Minoru replied without looking up.

"Are you sick? You aren't eating, you are not sleeping as you should; I hear you tossing during the night." When Minoru did not answer Joe tried again, "You are not worried about having tracked down your father, are you?"

"No. No, that has nothing to do with it."

"Well then, what is it? I know something is wrong."

"We've begun the study of the human body. I suppose I just can't accept the fact of Death. It is shocking to me, the cadaver, I mean. I am wondering now if I am fitted to become a doctor."

"Of course you are cut out for a doctor. All your life you've planned to be one, haven't you? *I know* I couldn't be one, but you will make a dandy. Stop worrying about it."

Minoru was silent for a long while, then said, "Joe, what is Life? What is Death? What is the meaning of it all?"

It was Joe's time for silence. In all of his life no one had asked such a thing of him and he was not prepared to deal with it now.

"You think too much, Minoru. At least you are doing too much thinking now. Were I in your shoes, I suppose I would be thinking, too, but I'm so busy living Life that I haven't thought much about its source, its end or its direction. I'm sorry. I'm not capable of answering your questions."

"Do you think that life is all chance, or do you think there is design?" Minoru continued to probe. Joe did not try to answer this. Minoru tried again, "Back of it all do you think that there is a Creator? Intelligence? God?"

"Yes, in a vague sort of way, I believe there is a God. My folks are Christians, and believe that God *is* and that He sent Jesus into the world to reveal Himself to men. Some of this has rubbed off on me, but not very much. At least, I don't believe it deeply enough to try to make you believe it."

"Do you believe that Life ceases when the body returns to dust?" Minoru was not letting him out of facing things.

"I don't know what I think, Minoru. My folks believe that there is a life after death. They believe in both Heaven and Hell, but I don't. I just never think about it."

"You are fortunate, but I *must* think. It is before me all the time."

They spoke no more about this that night or later, but Minoru continued to worry. Questions swarmed his mind like mosquitoes over an open ditch: What is life? What is its source? For what purpose do we live? Back of it all is there design? Intelligence? God? After the breath of life has gone, what then?

Since the other medical students were going through the same experiences and were keeping their thoughts to themselves, Minoru kept at the study until his mind and emotions adjusted and dissecting was no longer repulsive to him. After this gruelling stretch of study he definitely decided to become a surgeon.

It was this time that he met Toshio again and invited him home for dinner. Joe was to be absent, and Toshio would make an excellent substitute for him, besides, he wanted to have a good talk with his old friend.

"Are you still going to Mrs. Grady for English lessons?" Minoru asked, after Obasan had removed their dinner tray and brought a kettle of water to put over the coals for fresh tea.

"Yes. I wouldn't miss it. She is my recreation for the week. You will think me crazy, Minoru, but since I saw you last, I have accepted Christianity. I don't understand much about it yet, but Mrs. Grady is patiently teaching me and I am studying the Bible for myself. I wish that you would join her class too, Minoru."

"Toshio, this business of getting to be a doctor is a full time job. I *never* have time for anything else. But let me say, I don't think you crazy. I almost envy you — not for being a Christian particularly — but for having some satisfactory philosophy of life upon which you are working. I feel the need dreadfully."

"Try to study the Bible which Mrs. Grady gave you. Sometimes it speaks to the heart. It is the word of *Life.*"

Minoru did not understand such talk — it smacked of mysticism. He turned the conversation to other matters.

Before either Joe or Minoru realized it, school was over and Joe was packing for returning to Eugene, Oregon. As he packed, he talked constantly of friends and family at home. It was as if his mind had run home ahead of his person. Joe was filled with happy anticipation but Minoru dreaded to think of parting with his friend. He managed to get time off from school to go with Joe as far as Yokohama to see him sail away.

At Nishinomiya station, waiting to board the fast express to Yokohama, Joe's school boys and some members of the school faculty were crowded upon the platform when the train steamed into the station and glided to a stop. Minoru entered the train with Joe, carrying as many bags as possible so that his friend could acknowledge the good-bys being shouted to him.

Joe waved to them from the train window as the train quickened its speed and left them a dark blur upon the station platform.

In Yokohama, Minoru tried not to let his sorrow over the parting show. He had never had a friend like Joe Harden. It was a special friendship which would always live in his memory.

"Please, Joe, write to me often," Minoru begged. "I'll promise to answer, no matter how much work piles up on me. We must keep in touch, and when I get to America, I promise to see you first of all."

"I promise, Minoru. Give my love to Obasan." Joe slapped Minoru affectionately on the shoulder and turned toward the gangplank to board his ship for home.

Minoru stood on the pier watching the big liner being tugged out of the harbor, into the Pacific Ocean and wished that he were going too. Waving, even after he could no longer see Joe at the rail, he watched the ship fade into the sunset-flooded sky and the fast-fading light turned into a dim mist, a mere step from darkness.

Before Minoru realized it, he was caught up in his year of internship in the great, sprawling hospital in Kyoto. He knew now that his niche in life was definitely medicine, and these days for him were adventurous and profitable in continuous learning. For two years he had been subscribing to the chief medical journals of both America and Germany. These he studied assiduously, and, from them, learned many new methods of surgery which he wished to have the liberty of trying out on his patients. However, he knew enough of professional jealousies to soft pedal his desires. Many of his professors believed that the old methods were good enough. Some of the old ones would have sneered at the idea of his reading foreign journals to seek new methods. Foreign ways were for foreigners; Japanese methods of doing things were best for Japanese.

As long as he worked under their strict supervision, Minoru determined to abide by their decisions and directions, but this did not make him cease his research for better methods and to keep abreast of every up-to-the minute method reported in the journals.

The day before the final graduation from the Medical College, Minoru was sent a formal invitation to appear before the Hospital Governing Board. When he entered the long room and saw the illustrious gathering about the long table, and was led to a seat among them, he did not know what to make of it. He quietly took his seat and looked about him, wondering and a bit embarrassed.

The chief of surgeons rose to make a little speech and Minoru sensed all eyes of those assembled were now turned to him. He was told that through his years with the medical center, Minoru Tada had been stamped as a man who would make his mark on the medical world in the field of surgery. Believing that he could make a decided contribution to medicine in Japan, they were offering him a place on the Staff of Surgeons as instructor as well as practicing surgeon.

Minoru was stunned by such a sudden offer. Without a word, he rose and went to stand by the window, looking at the huge building spaced about the crowded campus where he had spent his last six years of study, thinking of all the medical students, now hurrying here and there across the campus, who would jump at such a chance as had just been held out to him.

One part of Minoru wanted to jump, too, accept the offer with thanks and settle down to a life of surgery in this bee-hive of a place; the other part of him refused to relinquish the dream of getting to America. There was a little matter of business to be settled there — a debt of vengeance which had to be paid. As he stood weighing these things, he wondered which really was the greater reason for holding to his dream: carrying out the oath of his youth or getting the graduate work which would make of him the best possible surgeon. Here for the first time, with this offer which would cancel out both of these desires, he was conscious of another thing, to carry out one of his resolves in America might erase the chance for the other. For a moment he was tempted to turn his back on the American venture and deliberately plant his life here. These men, who waited patiently for his answer, would give him a chance to weigh things. With this in mind, he turned back to the table and remained standing behind his chair.

"Gentlemen," he heard his own voice saying, "I am both humbled and flattered by such an offer by this group." He paused, dropped his eyes, and almost against his will said softly, "but I must reject it. For years I have planned to go to America for graduate study. I am sure I can become a better surgeon for a year or two of study there. Fortunately, I have the means to finance it as well as time to study. I feel that I must therefore reject your offer, but I do so with regrets."

When he sat down, and looked about him he saw consternation written on all faces except Dr. Sanda's. He was the first to speak.

"The fact that this position was offered to you, Dr. Tada, (How good the title sounded to Minoru at this point!) is proof of what we think of your potential as a surgeon. In this day, when methods are changing in the field of medicine, in surgery particularly, I feel that you are wise in rejecting the offer. The fact that you *do* have the means and time for such a venture is fortunate indeed. So often, those who have the ability do not have the means to follow through; those who have the means do not have the ambition. Yours is a happy combination. Congratulations."

In the eyes of the other members of the Medical Board, Minoru read a slight contempt. He instinctively knew what some of them were thinking: that it was his foreign strain which was pulling him to America. But, for once in his life, such thoughts mattered not at all. Let them think what they wished to think; he would exercise the same privilege.

Two days after turning down the offer to work on the Medical College staff, Minoru received a letter; one glance at it made him sink upon the nearest zabuton in the living room, and sit holding the letter unopened in his hand.

During the past two years he had written many letters to query American Medical Centers concerning the possibility of obtaining a fellowship for future study. Already he had answers from most of them; some had rejected his application outright; others had left the door open for further correspondence. At two of the places he had been accepted as a graduate student but the financial responsibility, they wrote him, would be his own. From the center where his illustrious father was chief of surgeons he had heard nothing. For some reason he had been secretly glad that his application there had been ignored. He felt that to be near the despised man would be a decided handicap, and at this point he wanted nothing to interfere with his studies.

Now, whether or not he wanted the letter, it had at last come. His hands holding it were shaking with nervousness. He wondered if it would not be wise to put it unread into the trash can. His curiosity was too strong for that. After all, they might have turned him down, as some of the others had done.

He tore open the letter hastily and read:

Dear Dr. Tada:

Your letter and application for graduate study here at the Medical Center was received several months ago. We are sorry to be so late in answering it but there were many such applications; to examine them all has taken time.

We have carefully checked your records and credentials sent with your application and we are happy to tell you that one of the available fellowships has been awarded to you. Congratulations.

We should like to have your acceptance as soon as possible. We are cognizant that the date September 19th may push you but it is the best we can do. If there is anything we can do to facilitate things for you on this end of the line, let us know. We hope nothing will hinder your coming to us this September.

Sincerely,

Minoru continued to hold the letter as he sat deep in thought. For just a moment he felt as if Fate had taken a firm hand. The thing he had wished and planned for so long was now within his reach, and he was not sure he wanted it. Yet, how could he reject it? There were enough funds in his estate to make it possible without financial help, yet the American venture might leave him stripped, when such funds as he possessed might better be used to build and equip his own offices, or for a small beginning of a hospital which he eventually hoped to build. This was the only place which had offered full financial backing.

He felt the blood thumping in his temples; a chill lay in his heart. He would blank his mind to his father, try to forget all about him for awhile, and to count himself fortunate in having been given this generous offer.

I will get this letter off before there is time to argue myself out of the whole thing. I'd be a fool not to know when I am well off.

He read over his reply, quickly put it into the envelope and sealed it for tomorrow's posting. Having finished this, his qualms subsided and he began to plan his next steps in getting ready to depart for America in late August.

Next morning after breakfast, he called Obasan into his room and outlined his future plans to her. It had always been her part to listen to things he said, without comment, then follow through without question. This time she sat before him weeping silently as she listened.

"You will stay here, Obasan, to take care of everything while I am away. I shall see that there is enough money for your needs each month and you may invite your niece to come to be with you for company. Maybe with a girl in the house, you will be waited upon for a change. That would be something, wouldn't it?"

She did not respond to the humor of this but continued to weep. Looking at her there in a huddle of misery at the thought of parting, Minoru realized that this separation would be a final break with familiar living for her.

"America is very far away, Minoru, and I shall be lonely without you here for me to look after. I may never see you again."

"Oh, yes you will. You will be right here to welcome me home again. Time will pass quickly, and I will keep letters coming to inform you of how things are with me, and be back for you to wait on before you really get rested."

The old woman gave him a sad, slow smile through her tears.

"All that may be true, Minoru, but who will look after *you* in that strange place?"

Minoru could not answer at once. Who would look after him indeed? He had not once thought of that. Obasan had made his life so very comfortable, for one swift moment he was sorry he had planned to go through with this idea of foreign study, and ultimate revenge!

12

JOE HARDEN HAD kept his promise to write after getting home to America, so Minoru felt that neither of them would find the other greatly changed after their two-year separation.

As Minoru hurriedly made plans for getting off to America, he sent a hurried appeal to Joe for help.

Joe: I have been advised by the Medical Center that my meals will be furnished from the cafeteria, but my place to live must be of my own choosing. This seems an impossible task for me. Could you help? May I leave everything in your hands?

In a great hurry, Minoru.

Before he set out from his home in Takarazuka, a reply came from Joe that put his mind at rest. Things had been arranged. With this assurance from his friend, Minoru set out on the long journey across the world.

It had been Joe's suggestion that he meet the boat in Seattle and they spend the first night together in a hotel of Joe's choosing. Minoru stood by the ship's rail, day after day, as if he could hasten the speed toward Seattle. He had much time to think of his American friend, and of the good fortune that was his that day, three years ago, when he had by chance seated himself beside the leggy American youth. *Without Joe I would never have traced Dr. David McLean, and without that, I doubt that I should have applied for graduate study abroad.*

When the liner finally eased into its berth at Seattle, Minoru found himself as excited as a child. Midway on the debarking stairs, he paused to search for Joe in the milling crowd below; just as he saw him flailing his arm in welcome, someone rudely gave Minoru a shove from the rear. He quickened his descent.

How wonderful and how simple everything now seems with Joe down there to welcome me.

When Minoru's foot touched the pier, Joe reached to take his hand, and draw him away from the crowd. He stood pounding Minoru's back in welcome, chatting as fast as he always had. Minoru accepted this exuberance with true Oriental patience and dignity, letting Joe guide him through the confusion into the customs office.

That evening in the hotel dining room Minoru still seemed to feel the long swells of the ocean beneath him but that in no way dulled the sharp edge of his pleasure at being with his friend, nor kept him from enjoying the delicious meal. He felt happy, secure and infinitely thankful.

They waited until they were in their hotel room before attempting to get down to the business of catching up on the news of each other. They talked the evening hours away. "Tell me about Obasan, Minoru. Did she say how happy she was when the big foreigner removed himself from underfoot?"

Minoru laughed. "Never, Joe. Obasan likes you very much and missed you when you left us. She sent you her yoroshiku (regards). She often says when she serves my tray, 'That Joe Sama should be here to eat with us tonight. He did not like all that I prepared, but he would like *this*.' "

"Bless her old heart. You know, Minoru, I envied you having her to look after you. How lucky can one get?"

Before they finally decided to call it a day and get to their rest, Joe asked frankly, "Minoru, now that you are actually headed to the place where your illustrious father abides, exactly what are your plans with regard to him? Another thing, how in the world did you arrange to get in the same Medical Center with *him?* That beats me."

Minoru was silent for a moment. Joe noticed the perspiration edging his broad brow and the white spots about his distended nostrils.

"I will answer the last question first, Joe. I *can't* explain how I got the fellowship. I do not believe in the Fates, but it seems that they must have been a bit busy for me. How else can it be explained? The other Medical Centers which answered my queries, had either turned me down or expressed little interest in me. Only the Western Center made a definite offer of a fellowship plus an allowance besides. Queer thing, too, I had almost forgotten I had applied there, for I'd become convinced that I'd really prefer not to hear from them; I certainly was not too keen to study there. Just as I had marked them off on my list, a letter came with the wonderful offer. What could I do but accept?"

"You'd have been foolish to have refused it. Now, that answers number two, how about number one?"

"As to what my plans are about getting even with my father, I have none. All through my boyhood I hatched a million ways to make him suffer. In fact, I've spent long waking hours plotting them but I have never been able to come up with a concrete, satisfactory plan. Actually, I suppose it depends upon the sort of man I find him to be. I think I shall let events take care of themselves. Right now I am so happy about my good fortune in this chance to study, I can't come to grips with any 'act of revenge.' "

"Be careful, Minoru. You could easily lose this chance which has been handed you. It simply would not be worth it. But be sure to let me know of your first meeting with Dr. McLean. I'm going to wait bug-eyed with curiosity."

Joe told him then of the living arrangements which had been made for him.

"You are to live in the house of Mrs. Kenneth Wentworth, a lady who has, for years, opened her home only to foreign students at the Medical Center. She does it as a hobby; she does not need the money but feels that it is a contribution she can make. Mrs. Wentworth is a widow."

As Joe talked, Minoru's eyes grew wide with interest. Living in an American widow's home was going to be quite a venture for him. He thought of Toshio and Mrs. Grady, and, for a fleeting moment wished that Toshio were here to share some of this strangeness with him.

On the train headed East, Minoru could close his eyes and feel that he was on a fast express to Tokyo, but, when he opened them to view the great open spaces of the American scene, he had the feeling that he was in an uninhabited land. Nowhere had he seen so much unoccupied space. He thought of the problem of his own country, desperate for space, where bull-dozers were constantly busy biting off the tops of mountains to make room for the high rise apartment houses to absorb the frightening increase in population.

When the train rushed through the fertile Mid-west with its limitless fields of wheat and corn, he was amazed. As far as his eyes could see there were fields of wheat stubble; the corn was still standing row upon row ripening for the fall harvest.

The hours seemed to pass too rapidly for him. He knew that he was secretly dreading the arrival in Cleveland, Ohio. It would be his first time to make his own way in a strange world. His English was understandable, but he had already discovered that Americans, whom he questioned, always became so interested in looking at him, they forgot to listen to his heavily accented words.

Before the train glided to the stop, Minoru took out his little black book, and began to memorize the address of Mrs. Wentworth. He hoped that it would not be too far from the station by taxi and that he could make himself understood.

He followed the other passengers from the train out upon the wide platform, found a spot to put his bags about his feet and wait until he could get his bearings. As he turned toward the stairs leading to the exit, he saw an Oriental pushing his way toward him, so he waited, and thought, *This man is not a Japanese; he is either Korean or Hawaiian.*

"I am Samuel Kim," the young man approached with his hand outstretched in welcome. "And you are Minoru Tada?" he asked.

"Yes," Minoru was able to say, relief and pleasure shining on his face.

"Miss Julia sent me to meet you," Kim said.

"Yes, yes, thank you. Miss Went-wurth, yes, yes, I understand. You live there too?"

"Yes, I do and you are our newest addition," Kim told him as he called a red-cap to carry the bags down. "Miss Julia thinks of everything to make us feel at home."

In less than an hour, they were unloading Minoru's bags before an old red brick mansion, the like of which Minoru had never seen. He let his eyes follow the stately lines of this mid-nineteenth century home, and wondered fleetingly how anyone could have conceived such a dwelling: rounded turrets, curving window panes and a wide porch which seemed to flow about the front of the house.

Kim led him into the house as if it were his own home. Minoru followed him into the cavernous foyer and looked furtively about the wide rooms which opened from it. Into the dim interior, the slanting rays of the afternoon sun sifted through the tall, brocade-draped windows. His first impression was one of being crowded by things even in the midst of space. He was suddenly homesick for the simplicity of his Japanese home.

A tall woman in her late fifties appeared from the back of the house to greet him.

"Welcome to your American home, Dr. Tada." Even her voice seemed to envelope him with a comforting warmth. She then turned to Kim. "You found him without trouble, Kim? My, what a find he is!" She turned her large gray eyes toward Minoru and said in her forthright way, "You're a good looking young man, if I ever saw one. Welcome to our Oriental family. Most of us are Orientals this year. It just happens so, for, some years we are quite Occidental, then again we are sort of tutti-frutti." She laughed at her own words, Minoru smiled politely not knowing half of what she had said.

While she talked, he studied her as a very strange person in his experience. He noted her regal bearing and the out-going quality that made a stranger feel strange no more. Her iron gray hair was piled high on her head, giving her naturally long face a sort of horsey look so prized in the ladies of ancient Japan.

"Take him up to his room, Kim, please, and see that he has everything he needs. Tell him about the dinner tonight which will be in his honor."

Carrying two of the bags, Kim led the way up the curving stairs into a high ceilinged room with furnishings to match the era of the house. Minoru noticed with pleasure that the room was for one person only. He had always roomed alone, and found that he was most comfortable with only his books for company.

"Your bathroom, which you share with me, is here." Kim threw open one of three doors of the room. He explained that he was the honored guest at dinner tonight at Miss Julia's.

"Take your time to get settled. Dinner will be at 6:30. When you are ready, come on down to the den — the room below."

Minoru thanked Kim, and closed the door. He walked about, noting that this was a turret room, and even the walls were rounded. The curved panes of glass fascinated him as he stood for a time looking at the vista of the out-of-doors. Trees were everywhere, shutting off much of the view, but, on this hot September day, it gave him a feeling of coolness. The massive buildings beyond the court he judged to be the Medical Center. What better place could have been found for his years of study? He was filled with gratitude to Joe for finding such a convenient place.

Five other students besides himself sat about Miss Julia's table that evening. There was only one other new boy, for the others had completed their first year of study. Two of them were from Taiwan, two from Korea; the new boy was from the Philippines. After the introductions to his fellow housemates, Minoru sat observing all the newness about him: the damask-draped, oval table, the spaciousness of the room, the gleaming silver pieces on the chest, the large chandelier with its hundreds of prisms making the general effect one of brilliance. He listened to the easy chatter which went on in English, and realized that he would have to make much progress before he could join them in such a conversation.

He watched Miss Julia at the head of the table, presiding with dignity and thoughtfulness. Minoru kept watching for a servant or two to appear. When the time came for plates to be changed, two of the old boys took them to the kitchen. Miss Julia, he discovered, had prepared the meal; the boys helped her in serving it. This, for one who had been waited upon from his birth, was a strange twist of things indeed.

Snow had begun to fall, and winter had let down upon the world, before Minoru began to feel at home in this new situation. Little by little he was led through the mazes of the medical set-up. In time he found his niche and gradually became acquainted with the men who were to guide him. In the midst of all the stir and confusion, he realized one day, while crossing the campus, that not once in all those weeks had he given his illustrious father a thought. He wondered vaguely what his first encounter with him would be, and just what would be his reaction when it occurred. He dreaded it, and wished that he had never heard of the man.

As Minoru walked home on Saturday afternoon from the college, kicking aimlessly at the dried leaves which slithered across his path, he made a sudden decision. Since it was a free afternoon, and since he had no plans, he stopped by a telephone booth to look up the home address of Dr. David M. McLean.

Why should I not do a bit of scouting on my own in this great metropolis? It will certainly be of interest to know where my father lives. Often, before coming to America he had imagined walking up the steps to a great house and announcing to anyone who came to the door, "I have come to see my father, Dr. David McLean." He smiled over this childish plan, but even now the thought of the consternation it might cause, amused him.

He found the address, jotted it in his book and waited for a bus which would take him in that direction. Finally one came. He boarded it, noticing its direction as it passed the college, then curved up a hillside, winding toward an exclusive residential section. Through the winter-stripped trees he saw spacious homes dotted over the hill's slope. They were set far back from the road, the spacious lawns now seared with frost. He scanned the house numbers on the gates and when he was sure he was nearing the desired neighborhood, left the bus and began to stroll along as if he were a resident out for a walk. His heart beat high when he neared the house, which by his calculations should be his father's. He paused at the gate to read the name. As he did so, a sports car rolled down the driveway, paused cautiously before turning into the main road. There was just time enough to catch sight of the beautiful young girl at the wheel. She was too busy watching the road to risk even a glance at him. He watched her skillfully maneuver the car as it slid smoothly into the road and started down the hill.

"His daughter?" Minoru asked himself, then wondered if the doctor had a son also in his family.

After walking slowly by the house, he reversed his steps, and walked again before this broad, white brick structure built on firm, gracious lines. Minoru looked with deep appreciation at the lines of it, and found them pleasing to his artistic sense of rightness.

When he made the return bus trip to Miss Julia's he centered his attention upon the different architectural designs of the homes along the way. In Japan there was a traditional design for houses with variations only in size, but in America a man exercised his freedom in the way his house should look. It sometimes made for an incongruous appearance, but the freedom about the whole thing pleased Minoru.

Most of all he liked the absence of fences. He had never understood the Japanese love for enclosing their special plots. It was as if they have no desire to share their created beauty. The Americans, Minoru concluded by this observation, display an open-handedness, a liberality, as if they are pleased to have others enjoy their plots. During the bleak winter season, things seemed less lonely with all the fences down, Minoru concluded.

Suddenly in memory he was again walking along the familiar alley near his home. His grandfather was beside him, when suddenly the old man struck at the strange wire fence and spat contemptuously in the dirt.

What would Ojiisan say if he could see me now? Deep inside he was glad that the old man could never know.

13

BEFORE CHRISTMAS, Minoru returned to his room at Miss Julia's earlier than usual in the afternoon. He went into the den where the student-guests were free to gather, to read newspapers and magazines, or to catch up with each other after the day's grind. He heard voices in Miss Julia's room next door. Without trying to eavesdrop he could not help overhearing; plans for Christmas were in the air. The young girl's voice was like music to hear; there were twinkles in her laughter. Minoru did not try to understand the words she was saying, he listened only to the tones, the rise and fall of the happy, young voice.

When the door opened, Miss Julia came out followed by one of the loveliest girls Minoru had seen since coming to America. She was delicately built, and exquisitely colored — sun tanned with overtones of gold. It was as if someone had deliberately edged her golden-yellow with an artist's brush. Even her eyes had golden lights in them as she turned to look at Minoru seated in the big arm chair. He was startled; he knew that somewhere he had seen this girl before.

"Minoru," Miss Julia said, "I want you to meet my niece, Betsy. Betsy this is Minoru Tada from Japan. Betsy and I have been making Christmas plans. We see very little of each other until holidays, then we make up for lost time."

Minoru rose from his chair, and without offering to shake her hand, bowed from the waist in true Japanese manner. "I'm glad to meet you," he managed to say distinctly.

"Hello," Betsy dimpled up at him. "So you are from Japan?" This was said as a question, and Minoru could tell by her eyes that she scarcely believed it to be true. She *knew* that he was not truly Japanese.

"How are you liking America?" she asked him.

"I like it very much: so far, so good. I work, work, work all the time, but that is the reason I came here."

"What is your specialty?" she asked it as if she knew her way about in medicine.

"I am a fellow in the school of surgery."

"My father is a surgeon, too," she said off-handedly, "I'd have liked to study medicine, but Dad would not hear to it. He thinks there are far better things in store for a woman than becoming a doctor."

"We have many women doctors in Japan," Minoru answered, looking her over with eyes which could not believe the beauty they were seeing. "Women make excellent doctors — especially children's doctors. I don't think I know a woman surgeon."

"Oh, I don't want to be a surgeon. I'm too chicken for that, but I do think that I might make a good pediatrician."

Miss Julia saw her niece to the door and turned back to Minoru.

"Betsy is your niece?" Minoru asked, keeping his voice even. He was sure now that this was the young girl in the sports car he had seen drive from the McLean home in October. His heart was beating like a trip hammer in his chest.

"Yes, she's my only brother's child, and she is *his* only child. She's the apple of his eye. Do you know the meaning of apple of his eye?"

"I never heard it." Minoru answered.

"It means that she is the most precious of all his possessions. Betsy's mother died when she was still in high school. My brother has never remarried, so naturally his affections center upon this beautiful child, Betsy. He spoils her though — spoils her dreadfully."

"What do you mean — 'spoil' her?" Minoru asked, thankful that she kept talking to him.

"It means that he indulges her — gives her whatever she wants. No girl can really develop under such treatment. Did you notice the car she drives? That is an expensive Mercedes, though any small car might serve her purpose as well."

"Does your brother live near here?" Minoru had to keep the conversation going until he knew his suspicions were true.

"Not too far away. His home is up on Burbank Hill — one of the loveliest residential sections of our city. Someday, I will drive you there; it really is worth seeing.

"You may have met my brother at the Medical Center, Minoru. He is chief of surgeons there. If you have not seen him, then you will before long. Every medical student does come to know him before they leave — Dr. David McLean."

She said this with pride in her tone, "You'll admire him as all of his students do."

It was fortunate at that moment that Miss Julia's eyes were turned in another direction. The flush which at that moment suffused Minoru's face, would certainly have caused her to be alarmed.

He excused himself immediately and hurriedly mounted the stairs to his room. Once there, with the door closed, he went to stand by the window to watch the large snowflakes sift over the tree tops.

This sudden revelation, this meeting with Betsy McLean, had shaken him as nothing else had ever done.

My mother, too, was the apple of her father's eye, yet David McLean gave him not a thought. Now that I have met the apple of

David McLean's eye, why should I consider his feelings? This chance to get even is even better than any I could have possibly dreamed up. This is the answer to my long search! This is the chance in a million to deliver hurt for hurt! Personal devils seemed tearing at him. He was torn and almost beside himself, experiencing a side to his nature absolutely new to him. It was almost as if he had, in a twinkling of an eye, become another person — strange even to himself. The sane part of himself was not submerged entirely, but kept interjecting questions for consideration:

Do two wrongs always make a right? Do you want to ruin your excellent chances for medical advancement? Do you deliberately wish to throw an insurmountable barrier across your path at the time you are finding life so rewarding?

Then came the realization which froze him by its logic — had David McLean not helped to bring you into being, you could never have been the person you are. Have you thought of that? Betsy McLean, the object of your scheming, is your half sister. These two are the only living relatives that you have in the world.

He sat down suddenly upon the side of his bed, and clasped his head in his hands. The profound silence of the moment engulfed him; in his mind he could hear the voice of his grandfather saying, "I have hated too much in my life, Minoru. Don't spend your time in hating; it is a waste, it is destroying to yourself."

Utter confusion overcame him; his stomach contracted with pain of tension, and blood pounded his temples. Feeling dejected and alone, he knew that he could not remain in this room, unable to breathe or think. He put on his heavy coat and went to wander about in the snow. It was frightening not to be able to bring one's thoughts in tow, and to think controlled thoughts. He let his tired mind idle like an engine as he walked aimlessly across the campus, making brand new tracks in the freshly fallen snow.

In the cafeteria he found that his appetite had completely forsaken him. The mingled smells of the hot food, which at other times made his appetite quicken, tonight made him ill. He turned and went out upon the street to wander until he was exhausted and depleted in mind and body.

He did not remember how he reached Miss Julia's or made it to his room. He only remembered changing into his night clothes and falling into bed, a lump of aching misery.

During the week after this emotional turmoil, Minoru was to experience for the first time the wonderful healing power of work. He buried himself in it, shunning all companionship except his books. He longed for Toshio, for he felt a great need to confide in someone who would understand.

The library was a haven for him during the dark, gloomy evenings of winter. He loved the muted silence there, where he could be alone, yet knew that others were about him.

It was late March before he realized that spring was not far away. When buds began swelling on the elm trees on campus and all snow had disappeared except that which clung to the ground in the shady corners, Minoru suddenly realized that at this time Spring was actually coming to Takarazuka; the cherry blossoms would be bursting open in their frantic blooming. He had an overwhelming desire to be there to see it. He wondered if he would be able to hold himself to his studies until the end of the school year.

With these thoughts running through his mind, he was crossing the campus to his room, when a sleek red car glided to a stop beside him. Looking up suddenly he found Betsy McLean opening her car door beside him.

"Hop in, Dr. Tada. How about coming for a ride with me? This is the sort of day to blow the cobwebs from your mind."

On impulse, Minoru responded to her greeting, and slid into the seat beside her. She dimpled at him, and accelerated the machine which shot forward as she skillfully guided the car around the corner.

"What do you mean by cobwebs?" Minoru asked her.

"You know what spider webs are, don't you?" Minoru nodded.

"We call them cobwebs. When we think too much — work too hard with our minds, we sometimes say that we have cobwebs in the mind that need blowing away. Have you been working hard since I saw you last?"

"Yes, very hard. No doubt I have many cobwebs!" This he said while he thought, *I have worked hard to keep from hating you.*

He looked askance at this girl beside him, this object of his scheming, and knew that again his chance had come to get even. He also knew that the thing was not working according to his plans, for almost immediately, he felt comfortable with this girl. The day was lovely, the ride about the hills was a delightful change for him. He found himself enjoying this new experience with a beautiful American, his half-sister.

"Where would you like to go?" she asked him, glancing now and again at his handsome profile.

"I don't know places. Any place you like."

"Do you like mountains — little mountains, I mean?"

"Yes, very much, I like the mountains, little and large. All Japanese like mountains. We have mountains wherever we look in Japan. Japan is very beautiful; it is small but it is everywhere beautiful."

"I'd like to go to Japan someday. My father was there once studying some tropical disease or at least used that as an excuse. He loved it and says that some day we may go there together. He says that we'll fly over some spring when the cherry blossoms are in bloom."

"That time is now in my country." Minoru's face was aflame, but Betsy was too busy with the car to notice. As a true son of Japan, Minoru kept complete control of himself. "There, it is a beautiful time of the year. It makes me a little bit homesick."

Betsy laughed and looked quickly at this more than suntanned youth. *He looks like a Greek god,* she said to herself.

The car continued up the steep incline of the hillside. From the place where she brought the car to a stop, one could get a complete panoramic view of the city. They got out of the car to see and enjoy the view from all sides.

Talk, which always came easily to Betsy McLean, suddenly did not seem necessary in the company of this tall, naturally silent person. From the first afternoon that she had met Minoru Tada at Aunt Julia's, she decided that a mock affair with this half-blood Japanese might be a way of striking back at her father. Since her first meeting with Minoru she had spent weeks hatching a plan to ensnare the handsome Oriental. Her first try had brought results. Of course she would never be really serious about him, but to flirt with him a little could certainly be useful in bringing around her stubborn father.

Betsy was careful not to mention this ride with Minoru Tada to her father. She was well versed in managing him, of slipping up on his blind side to bring him to terms calculated to please herself.

There is such a thing as perfect timing, she schemed to herself, *and I want no flaw in this build up. One day I shall invite the handsome Oriental to dinner, and, when my father sees me playing up to this new conquest he will see many things in a different light. He will hit the ceiling and it will be fun! After a near thing with an Oriental, Bob Moreland will look rather well to Dr. David, or I don't know my father!*

There were many rides with young Dr. Tada during the warming spring days. Betsy had the feeling that it was going to be hard work to crack his "Eastern shell," as she termed it to herself; he was always polite, quiet, and only mildly interested in all that she said and there was a something in him she could not understand. She knew her own powers, though, and kept them aimed at him.

"Have you ever been in love, Minoru?" Betsy suddenly asked him one day.

"No. My life has been too full of study — preparing for my profession — to think of marriage. The time for choosing a wife will come after I am prepared for life," he told her matter-of-factly.

"Love does not work like that, Dr. Tada. One does not deliberately decide to fall in love and do it. It sneaks in like a thief in the night, and you find yourself powerless," she laughingly told him.

"We Japanese lock our doors very carefully, and keep a night watchman to be on guard for us while we sleep." This made Betsy laugh uproariously. Minoru was warmed by her appreciation of his quick wit.

A few evenings later, when they were attending a symphony together, and the lilting strains of the violins seemed to cry into the heart to stir longings for expression, Minoru suddenly felt Betsy's soft little hand in his own. He was at first shocked but responded to her advance by closing his long supple fingers about hers in a tight squeeze. She snuggled closer to him, pressing her body against his side in a way that he found entirely pleasing to his senses.

14

MISS JULIA WAS not blind to all that was taking place between her niece and the handsome Japanese doctor. She took note of Betsy's behavior and became alarmed over the rapid progress being made under her nose. She watched from the window when Betsy dropped Minoru at her door after their rides. Not once did she come into the house for a visit with her aunt, nor did she refer to her dates with the doctor when they did by chance meet.

In all the years that Miss Julia had had foreign students in her home, never had a problem of this sort presented itself. Betsy had never made a habit of running in and out of Miss Julia's home. She only came when she needed something which Aunt Julia could supply.

Miss Julia often worried about her niece — a young woman who had finished her education but was without occupation other than amusing herself. All of Betsy's best friends were now married and had homes and interests of their own. Julia wondered, now that things were taking this queer turn, if David had been right in staunchly opposing Betsy's attachment to Bob Moreland. At the time, she had sided with her brother. Now that this thing was looming on the horizon, Miss Julia wondered, if it were to be done over again, whether she would not be inclined to throw the complete responsibility on Betsy and let her work it out alone. **After** all, she had been twenty years old at the time.

Bob Moreland is a hard drinker, a man with considerable inherited wealth — but just the kind of person Betsy has always been thrown with. David should not have been greatly surprised that she made a choice from among the only group she has known. He should not have been surprised when she became engaged to him. Miss Julia let these thoughts run through her head as she sat doing needlepoint. She found herself confused and impatient, jerking at the thread as she worked.

It is far better to let young people make their own mistakes — chart their own course through life. In Betsy's case, David could not bring himself to stand aside. She's his only child. He felt that he couldn't stand aside and let her make a botch of her life which held so much promise. It just may be that he'll live to regret it, if this thing with Minoru Tada is on the level. It is very hard to judge Betsy on that score. Usually I can see through her little tricks when her father doesn't. It is unthinkable that she could be so addled as to allow herself to fall in love with a Japanese man. Minoru is a wonderful person, but, the fact remains, he is Japanese. Miss Julia was troubled. She wondered what steps she could take, if any, before the thing got completely out of hand.

Suddenly she remembered a scene which had happened in this very room, years ago, when a letter had come from David in Japan. Her mother had read the letter aloud almost shouting the lines in her frustration:

> It was by chance that I met Michiko Takahashi, a willow-wand of a girl and as graceful as anyone I've ever seen. Her skin is the color of a slightly bruised magnolia blossom and as soft. She is altogether lovely.
>
> She belongs to a good family and takes great pains that I have no chance to meet them. They would be as shocked as you are being as you read this letter.
>
> I am not in love with this girl, but I jolly well could be at the drop of a hat.

Never had Julia seen her mother in such a state. "Our son bringing home a Japanese wife! Over my dead body!"

Miss Julia remembered saying, "But, Mother, David is almost twenty-six years old. If he loves a Japanese girl, I should think that is his affair."

Her mother, too angry for words, took out her anger in looks at her daughter whose opinion had not been asked for. The father had said little, but he did later tell them that he'd be the one to answer the letter.

"It will do us no good to oppose David, Martha," he had said firmly. "He is old enough to know better, and we think he should have better sense. David has always been a sensible person, though this letter does not bear me out. He says that he is not in love with the girl. If he isn't, this is mighty silly talk. I shall write to point out a few problems that such a union would engender."

The father had never let them read the letter which he sent to his son. He had simply announced at the dinner table that the letter was on its way to Japan.

"What did you write him, Milton?" Mrs. McLean had asked.

"Plenty," was the father's only answer.

That had not been the end of the affair. David had written a few weeks later that he had decided to marry the girl and bring her home as his wife.

Miss Julia could not remember just what happened, but he had arrived home alone, and nothing more was said about the affair. So far as she now remembered nothing more was ever said about it.

This will be a pretty kettle of fish for Me to have to tell David *what is in the wind for his daughter. It's mostly her doings, for certainly Minoru never goes out of his way to contact Betsy. When they talk over the telephone, it is she who calls him.*

I wonder if David has met Minoru? Miss Julia sat punching her needle in and out of the tapestry as she worried with these thoughts, and to herself she suddenly said aloud, "I must *do* something. I can't just sit here!"

Miss Julia had never been one to interfere with another's affairs. *If only Martha were living; she would know what to do.*

Martha Westmoreland had been Julia's best friend before her marriage to David. Julia had always given herself credit for the match between her handsome brother and the girl whom he married after a hurried courtship soon after getting home from Japan. It had been unfortunate that Martha could not have given David a son. He had wanted one more than most men. At one time he had considered adopting one, but Martha had put her foot down.

Martha had found being a surgeon's wife a difficult position to fill. She was a society girl by birth and by preference, and a surgeon husband was not always available for an evening escort. Often Martha had confided in her sister-in-law,

"Just let me plan one evening out and that will be the time for Mrs. Gotrocks to have a kink in her intestines, or Mrs. Plushorse to come down with an attack of appendicitis. It's as sure as night following the day, Julia. I get really provoked at times."

Julia had felt during those days that David did not try hard enough to please Martha, or adjust to the family situation.

"Just be glad that you did not marry a practitioner," David would retort when the going got rough. "At least I can schedule operations most of the time, except for emergencies."

"But, oh the emergencies!" Martha would say.

Miss Julia realized that this day-dreaming was getting her nowhere. She rose resolutely from the chair, folded her needlepoint on the table beside her and went to the telephone. Without hesitating a minute, she dialed her brother's office.

"David, I want to have a talk with you as soon as you can arrange to see me," she said immediately after being connected with his inner-sanctum.

"What on earth has happened, Julia? You sound so mysterious."

"I can't tell you now, David, but I do think it important. When can you see me? I'd rather it be at a time when Betsy is not at home, for I think we'd better talk at your house rather than mine."

"Betsy is out tonight, at least she told me that she'd not be in for dinner. You know how I dislike eating alone — why don't you plan to have dinner with me tonight? Suppose I pick you up on my way home this afternoon — in about an hour say."

"I'd love to have dinner with you. Suits me fine. I'll be ready when you come by. Just toot."

After the doctor called to say that his sister would be his dinner guest, Mrs. Hayes, the McLean housekeeper and cook, outdid herself in the preparation of a good dinner for them. It was not elaborate, but her skill could make simple foods a feast. Dinner was the one meal of the day over which the busy doctor could linger; Mrs. Hayes always saw to it that it was a good one.

During the dinner hour the two of them were very gay, recalling old times, sharing news of mutual friends and relatives. Miss Julia did not touch upon the problem until they were seated before a small fire in the den. The bright spring day had ended in a sudden chill.

"You know, David, that I have made it a rule of my life never to interfere with your or Betsy's affairs, unless you ask my advice. It has made for excellent relationships, but in this matter, I feel that I am partially responsible. I hardly know how to begin.

"Do you know the Japanese doctor, Minoru Tada, who lives at my home?"

Her brother did not answer at once. He seemed to be reaching back into his mind for a face and a name to go with it.

"No, I can't actually say that I know him or have ever seen him. I remember the name, for I was the one on the committee who insisted that he be given the fellowship at the Medical Center. Why?"

"Do you know that your daughter has developed quite a crush on this Oriental and has been seeing him every chance he will give her? He is a handsome young man, but I am sure you do not approve of such a thing." While he sat in thoughtful silence, Miss Julia broke the tension by a head-tilting laugh.

"This is really quite funny, David, isn't it? It is like an old movie being refilmed with the background and the couple in reverse positions."

David McLean smiled a sad, slow smile. "You refer to my flare-up in Japan?" He put his hands against his temples and pressed them firmly.

"You are not sure that Betsy is serious about this young man, are you?"

"No, I'm not sure of anything concerning Betsy. Neither are you. I only watch their comings and goings; I have wondered where it is leading. I've said not a word to either of them. Betsy is very careful not to give me a chance to question her. I am sure that it is more of her affair than it is Minoru's. He's a serious student and unversed in American ways. I think he really does not know what it is all about."

"Oh, I remember the boy to whom you refer," David McLean said abruptly. "He is not fully Japanese — not full blooded, I mean. He could pass for a tall Spaniard so the professors tell me. I have not seen him. He is making his mark at the Center. The professors are watching him with great interest. Thanks for being frank with me, Julia. I'll have a talk with Betsy about this." He continued to smoke his pipe in silence, then said, more to himself than to his sister, "Could it be that Betsy is serious about this man?"

They turned the channel of conversation to other things until it was time for him to drive his sister home. On his return home he decided not to wait up for Betsy. He had long given up that habit, and it would be poor timing to discuss this thing with her tonight. He went straight to his room and prepared for a good night's rest. Once in bed, he tried to turn off the workings of his mind, but somehow the visit with Julia had set off a train of thoughts that he could not control — thoughts that he had not entertained in years.

How long had it been since he had relived those years and mistakes in his memory? Years ago he had forced himself to stop thinking about Michiko. It had always been painful, and made him feel guilty. To this day, he could not know what made him cut all the threads which bound him to her, and might have someday drawn him back to Japan. There were times when he wondered if she were still living and if she ever thought of him. Tonight, like bubbles of gas from puff-mud, these long-buried thoughts rose to his mind's surface and demanded his attention.

Lying in the darkness of his room, he confessed that the feelings he had experienced for that beautiful Japanese girl, he had experienced for no other person — not even for the woman who became his wife.

He lay remembering the sweet moments he had had with Michiko, the last meeting with her when he went to say good-by. He had told her that he had been ordered home, that his parents were not pleased with his plans, that he would return to marry her in the very near future after he had talked it over with his parents. These things were not true, but, to a Japanese mind, they made good sense. He had felt guilty ever since.

After he came home to America, the whole idyll had faded into the realm of dreams. Why should they come now to him with such force? Why could he not put them back into the realm of faded dreams?

It was because the young Japanese doctor was from Takarazuka that he had thrown his weight in favor of the fellowship for him, and had given him his chance for study in America. Had he been from another town, David McLean knew that his vote might have been cast for someone else. He had seen "Takarazuka" beside the applicant's name and had hardly looked at his credentials: He was dreaming of the little town nestled back in the mountains of the Kwansai. Now, this sentimental move on his part had boomeranged. History was repeating itself, and though he had long ago concluded that his parents were right in opposing his love affair, he wondered if he should present the same reasons to his daughter *if* she really cared for this young doctor, and he really cared for her. Minoru Tada plainly was a promising doctor, but there were other things to be considered and weighed.

He remembered his father's letter of a few words, but with each word packing a wallop.

> This girl may be as lovely as anything you have ever seen, my boy, but she still lives in another world from yours. Marriage has enough stumbling blocks at best without going out to look for others. Project yourself into the future — would you want your mixed-blood children to grow up here? Would you be proud to introduce them to your family and friends? Would they not always seem a bit strange to you? Maybe it would be a grave injustice to confuse their world even before they enter it.

> These are things for you to consider, David. The decisions must be your own. Common sense will tell you a great many things if you will exercise it. Even the birds — with their birdbrains, know to stick to their own kind.

David McLean smiled in the darkness, remembering how stupid

he had thought his father when the letter reached him in Japan. But, as he applied the same yardstick to his daughter's case, the words of his father seemed to make excellent good sense. He might well use them in his talk with Betsy tomorrow.

When he finally fell asleep, he dreamed that he was back in Takarazuka. It was cherry blossom time, and he was searching for something he could not find. He awoke tired and depleted of strength. The dream seemed to follow him through the day and his thoughts kept drifting on the winds of memory, making him sad and listless.

15

DAVID MCLEAN WAS not one to let things needing his attention go unattended; he believed in getting things done at once, so, the next morning he left a note on his daughter's breakfast plate.

> How about having dinner with me tonight — out? I'll even let you choose the place. Call me at the office to accept if you have nothing more important on your schedule. I will come home to dress; we'll go together from home.
>
> > Love you,
> > Dad.

Betsy found the note when she came down for breakfast in mid-morning. She was reading it when Mrs. Hayes came bringing her breakfast.

"U-u-um, Dad wants me to have dinner with him tonight, Marnie. Isn't that something? Maybe he wants to insure himself against one of my concoctions on your night off." They laughed together.

"No, that can't be the reason, for after his description of last week's dinner, I offered always to leave it prepared ready for you to heat up. Maybe it is because he wants to see more of his daughter than he's been doing lately."

Marnie was good at such snide remarks and Betsy was used to her way of dishing them out to her. She let Mrs. Hayes talk while she continued placing things about her on the table. When she finally left to continue her morning chores, Betsy began to wonder about the sudden invitation. Was there something he wanted to discuss with her? It couldn't be about Minoru Tada, for he knew nothing about that. Since it was a ruse to displease her dad she was not ready to spring this upon him. She would first have to be sure that Minoru had fallen in love with her. Anyone could see by a glance at him now that he was far from that. She felt, at the moment, that to make him do so was in her power, and that too would have to be timed correctly.

Bob Moreland is still hanging high for my picking. I know I can call him back to me whenever I please, but I must not wait too long. After this affair with Minoru Tada, Dad will be quite willing to come to terms. I'll take time to make plain to him that he can never again dictate the terms as he did before.

Mrs. Hayes came back to bring the jelly, which she had forgotten, and broke into Betsy's thoughts.

"Your Aunt Julia was here for dinner with your father yesterday. Did he tell you?"

"No, not in his note. I haven't seen him since Saturday so he couldn't have told me. What was the occasion?"

"He called to tell me that she would join him for dinner; that was all. I wish that she would come more often. They had such a jolly time of it. Your father is lonely; I wish he would marry again — that's what I wish!"

Mrs. Hayes liked to drop these tiny bombs on the self-centered daughter of the house. Having let this one fall, she waited for the explosion. It came.

"Married again! Well I certainly want nothing of the kind. Whatever put such a thought into your head, Marnie Hayes?"

"Oh, nothing. It's just that I get sorry for him at times. He's a young man yet." Betsy snorted at this, but Mrs. Hayes continued, "It's true. Fifty-five is a good age; too young to think of spending the rest of his life alone. He needs more companionship than *you* give him, young lady, more than you *can* give him, in fact."

Saying this, Mrs. Hayes gave a cluck with her tongue which Betsy understood, from long years of hearing it, that was her final conclusion and any argument against it on anyone's part would be futile. Betsy knew better than to try. Mrs. Hayes flounced out of the room like an army with banners.

As soon as Betsy had finished her breakfast, she went to her room to call her father and to accept his dinner invitation that evening.

"How do you want me to dress tonight? Real prettied up or just so-so?" she asked him.

"Let's make it fancy. It isn't often that I have the pleasure of having my beautiful daughter with me when I step out, so let's do it up brown. I'll come home early so I'll have a chance to pretty up too. Glad you can go with me, Honey."

Betsy chose the swankiest place in the city for dinner. At the candlelit table, David watched his daughter and wondered where he had failed with this beautiful creature. Looking at her, he found it hard to believe that she would lose her head over a person like Minoru Tada. *What would life be for her in Japan? How could anyone, as sheltered and spoiled as she, ever hope to adjust to anything except the soft nest which only money, and plenty of it, can buy?*

These were his thoughts as he tried to center his attention on all that Betsy kept saying. Plainly this was her setting, and she was soaking it up.

In the darkness and closeness of the car going home, he thought of a way to open the discussion which would not make her throw out her porcupine quills at his first words.

"Where have you been keeping yourself lately? I've hardly seen you for days. I've called home several times to have you meet me down town. Always Mrs. H. says, 'She's gone somewhere in her car.' Any new conquests that I should know about, or should I wait for you to tell me?"

"Ah-ha, I knew it! Aunt Julia was over for dinner with you yesterday, wasn't she? I knew that she would leak to you about my seeing Minoru Tada. She did tell you, didn't she?"

"Yes, she did, and when we get home, we'd better discuss this. Now don't go blaming your Aunt Julia for tattling. You know that she is not that kind. She did not want to tell me; she hoped that you had."

"I was going to tell you when I felt the time was ripe. I have been seeing him every chance he will give me." She snuggled deeper in her mink stole, and, firmly believing that she was tightening the screws about his heart, said, "If you want the truth, I'm really quite smitten with this tall Oriental. Have you spotted him yet at the Medical Center?"

Her father's voice was calm and unruffled, "I may have seen him, but not to know who he is. He is a brilliant student, so the professors tell me, outstanding in fact, but there are other things to consider, Honey."

After this, each of them remained silent, thinking his own thoughts. Betsy's were baffled ones; this thing was not working according to her plan: David McLean was wondering if there were such a thing as having ones "chickens come home to roost." It was as Julia had expressed it, an old movie with but slight changes.

They did not speak of the matter again until they were in the den with the bright overhead lights on. Facing each other across the room Betsy had her lines well drawn, ready for a royal battle; armed for the attack.

"You might as well face it, Dad, I am in love with Dr. Minoru Tada. He is the most fascinating man I've ever met, and one of the most handsome."

She paused for this blow to fall; it did not. He answered gently, but with a worried crease between his eyes. "Is the man in love with you, Betsy?"

This almost took the wind out of her sails; it was so unexpected.

"Of course he is!" This she said implying, "Who could help being in love with me?"

"Have you thought of all the insurmountable obstacles which lie in your path of happiness?" he asked without lifting his voice.

"I can't see any 'insurmountable obstacles' as you call them. You said yourself that he is making an enviable record in medicine. Doesn't that please you?"

"Of course you know that Dr. Tada is not a full-blooded Japanese, Betsy, yet he bears a Japanese name. He probably is an illegitimate child; would that make a difference to you?"

Betsy was sure that she had him on the thorn here. "If I am sure that I'm in love with him, I'm not sure that it would matter one bit." This was hitting below the belt, and the flush in her father's controlled face told her so.

She had misinterpreted the expression on his face. David McLean suddenly realized that he had reached a point beyond which he must never again go with his headstrong daughter. The last time he had almost lost her; he would never be guilty of pitting his will against hers again.

"What if Dr. Tada should insist on carrying you off to Japan to live?"

"Folks do manage to live in Japan, Dad." Her voice was light and flippant.

"Have you any idea what life would be like for you, a foreign woman, where the place of woman is still rather lower than that for the man?"

"I know nothing except what you told me about the place. You loved it; remember? I've heard you say so."

"Now that was quite a different matter, Betsy. I did find the time I spent there very pleasant. I loved the beauty of the place, but I certainly never entertained any idea of staying permanently."

"I'm twenty-two years old, Dad." (This was the prepared speech.) "The last time I was in love, you dictated the terms. Never again! I will not let you do it. You must let me follow the dictates of my own reasoning." (She wondered if she were not overplaying her part.)

"What you say is true, Betsy. You are certainly old enough now to know your own mind. But, may I tell you a few things that you may not have thought about? Marital happiness is a tricky thing at best. In the case of Bob Moreland, I knew, if you didn't, that your chances of happiness were licked from the beginning. There could have been no happiness with one who has deliberately set for himself the shallow goal of pure pleasure. This is not true of Dr. Tada. He is a worthy young man in any country, but you *do* belong to different worlds. But, my child, if you truly know what things you will have to face, and you think that you can face them, then you have my blessings. I will leave things in your own hands, and to your own judgment."

Once, when Betsy was a child she had possessed a rubber doll, inflated like a balloon when filled with air. When the stopper in one of its feet was removed, the doll instantly became a flabby piece of rubber in her hand. At this moment she felt a kinship with that piece of rubber which had been a doll. Her father's words had removed the stopper of her ego; she was completely deflated. She had expected him to blow his top, and for this she had worked herself up for a glorious fight in which she would emerge victorious. It infuriated her to think that her father would consent to her marrying Minoru Tada. *It could be that Dad saw through my bluff and called it. I will show him!*

16

As Minoru entered the house one afternoon, Miss Julia called to him from the reception room.

"Is that you, Minoru? If it is, please come in here a minute; I need your tall help."

Minoru went to her immediately to find her standing on a chair, trying to straighten one of the large portraits on the wall. He took the picture into his own hands, and following her directions, hung it to her satisfaction. Minoru had never been in this particular room; now he took a few minutes to look about him.

"Nothing disturbs me like a crooked picture, unless it is a crooked mirror," Miss Julia told him. "Thanks for the help, Minoru, I should know by now not to try such a stunt when I am alone."

"So glad I came in just in time. Who are the folks in these portraits?" he asked as he made a swinging gesture with his hand about the room.

"Various members of the family. These two are our mother and father. Father had them painted soon after they moved into this house as bride and groom. David and I were born and grew up here."

Minoru concentrated upon his American grandparents for one long piercing moment while some new identity surged through his being. Miss Julia continued to talk.

"After Mr. Wentworth, my husband, died, I came back to this house to look after Mother. She lived to be quite an old lady. I've left everything just as it has always been." Miss Julia moved over to the opposite wall.

"These two gentlemen are my grandfather and his brother, Thomas. They are Scotsmen, and these must have been painted directly after they came to this country, for, in these paintings, they are still young men."

Miss Julia turned suddenly to look at Minoru to find him flushed of face, and smiling broadly over the new revelation of himself — *Scottish blood coursing through my veins!*

This new revelation gave him a distorted feeling, like being stretched around the globe.

"Having portraits hanging on our walls must be strange to you, Minoru. I understand the Japanese do not display their pictures so."

"Yes, it is so. The pictures of the family are kept in a place apart. We display paintings, but then, only one at a time."

Minoru was glad that Miss Julia was no longer standing near him; his heart was going like a drum's beat in his chest. He was sure that, were she near him, she could hear them. *These are my forefathers! These queer looking people are my relatives, as are Miss Julia and Betsy.*

He felt for the moment that his head would explode with this sudden knowledge.

"Is there a portrait of your brother, Dr. McLean?" he asked, keeping his voice even, with just the right shade of interest.

"Let me see. Yes, I *do* have a photograph of him, but no portrait." She stepped into the hall and returned bringing a framed picture in her hands. "This is a recent picture of him. Isn't he stunning? But you should have seen him as a young man. I thought my brother was the handsomest man in all the world at that time. He is still handsome, as you can see."

Minoru was afraid to stand before her looking at the picture for fear that even she might catch a likeness which was certainly there for anyone to see. He walked away from her to stand beside the window, to study more closely the picture in his hands. He could see much of his own face in it; there was a striking resemblance about the brow and the set of the eyes.

"He is indeed a handsome man, Miss Julia," he told her, *and, he was handsome in his youth too. I have a picture to prove it,* he would have liked to say to her.

"I have not yet seen your brother, but his lectures are scheduled for this month. I shall meet him then." He turned to replace the picture on the hall desk and excused himself to go to his room. There, he flung himself upon the bed, and made no move to turn to his studies. Too much strangeness had been handed him by his Aunt below the stairs. He felt that it would take a lifetime to assimilate all of it.

I am actually living in my grandfather's house in America. This house is as much mine as it is Betsy McLean's.

He got up from the bed and walked to examine his face in the mirror. *In some respects I am more handsome than my father, in a darkish kind of way. Were I as fair as he, anyone might see the likeness. I had never thought that I'd look like him! My idea of him has been so distorted by hate, I'll have quite a bit of adjusting to do.*

My father lived in this house, in this very room perhaps, looked at this view from this window, walked up and down the carpeted stairs and sat about the dining table beneath the gleaming chandelier!

In his dreams that night, he stood again looking at the framed photograph of his father. Suddenly the distinguished man, with white showing above his temples, broke into a broad grin, "Hi, Son," it said to him, "What in the world are you doing here?"

Minoru awoke from the dream filled with the wonder of it. "Could anything so wonderful as this happen in such a hateful, awkward situation?" he asked aloud in the early dawn. Lying in the bed thinking over much that had happened to him of late, he made a resolution. He would not see Betsy again. Things were getting out of hand, and he no longer had the desire to harm her. In fact, he was beginning to worry over his headstrong half-sister. She was a unique person in his experience. He knew that it was wise for him to make the break.

One afternoon, Minoru swung through the revolving door into the Medical Library to see his distinguished father standing by the front desk in conversation with the librarian. He froze in his tracks with astonishment, then quickly stepped between the book stacks where he could see without being seen. Within his being, there was a surprising surge of affection for this man who had given him life; something in Minoru cried out for recognition, like water seeking its level or the leap of an infant at the sight of its mother. Tears flooded his eyes as he turned away carrying with him this image of his father as something warm and greatly prized.

As Spring slowly returned to earth, Betsy found it almost impossible to contact Minoru Tada: he was too busy for a ride, work was piling up on him, there were hours to be spent in the dissecting laboratory. Betsy knew that this was not all the truth and she was frustrated by the seeming lack of interest.

At first she blamed Aunt Julia. When she confronted her Aunt with the accusation, she was told in no uncertain terms, "The only comment I have made to anyone about your seeing this Japanese doctor was to your father. I tell you frankly, Betsy, that I think it outrageous, for it *is* you who has chased — not he. If I thought for a minute that he were interested in you, I'd be more upset than I now am. I've said not a word to him, that you must believe."

Betsy did believe it but she was too stubborn to give up. She waylaid Minoru on his way home the next evening, slid her car to a stop beside him on the walk, and opened the door. When he refused to get in she let her temper flare, and accused him of deliberately avoiding her.

Minoru did not deny it. He smiled politely and pleaded a press for time, then spoke with surprising frankness.

"I do think it best not to see you again, Betsy. We might grow too fond of one another. I want to be your friend, nothing more. It would *never* do."

Then, as if to try to establish a new relationship he said,

"I saw your father the other day. He is a great doctor; you must be very proud of him."

Betsy looked at him with contempt in her eyes. "You must come to know my father. He *is* quite a guy." She started the car engine, and, without looking back, sped on her way.

On the ride home, Betsy began to put her findings together and come up with a deep suspicion. *No wonder Daddy was so calm over my admitted liking for the Oriental. He had already sought him out and let him know that any sort of relationship with his daughter is forbidden. Boy, he really fixed things for me! That ambitious Oriental would do nothing to lessen his chances of advancement at this Medical Center. So — my little playhouse is in shambles! My father has outwitted me.*

With this conjecture in her mind, Betsy was furious, that Aunt Julia had meddled, that her father would be so underhanded, and that Minoru would buckle under to his absorbing ambition. This anger she let smolder at home.

David McLean watched his angry daughter, saw her restlessness, and wondered what had gone wrong. He kept his silence and his temper; acted as if he were oblivious to the turmoil which raged within her. Once he dared ask if she would care to invite the young Doctor Tada to dinner with them. Her tart reply made him know that the affair with the young Japanese was not progressing satisfactorily.

In late May, David McLean was happy when his daughter came to say that she would like to go abroad with friends for the summer. This was a sign that the affair was over, and she was turning her thoughts to other conquests. He took a deep breath — a sigh of relief. There would be at least a lull between this crisis and the next one. Glad for the bit of respite which her trip abroad would afford him, he was only too happy to give his permission as well as the price of the tour.

After Betsy had sailed, Dr. David McLean gave one of his rare lectures to graduate students of surgery. Minoru sat in the amphitheater with his eyes riveted on the face of the lecturer. A feeling of pride in his father filled him. He was surprised that the students sitting near him could not sense all that he was experiencing at this moment. Then he realized that he alone in the audience was not giving his undivided attention to the instruction being given by the lecturer. Immediately he corralled his roving thoughts and concentrated them on all that was being said.

After the lecture was over, it was as if the teacher delayed his departure from the room until Minoru neared the door where he was standing. He seemed to make a point of singling Minoru out to discuss with him a point or two made in the lecture.

The young Japanese was flustered by this bit of special attention, but David McLean felt that he was ill at ease because of his relationship with his daughter, or perhaps because it was not customary for a Japanese student to talk on equal terms with a "Sensei" (teacher). David McLean tried to put this blushing man at ease by taking his arm and steering him into a small private office. There seated across the table from him, he thoughtfully studied this beautiful specimen of manhood and realized it *would* be possible for a girl like Betsy to lose her heart to him.

"My Betsy sailed for Europe this week to be gone all summer," he stated, watching the young doctor's reaction.

The young man's face reflected nothing of surprise, only slight interest in the announcement.

"Sō desu ka? (Is that so?) I have been so busy, I did not even know that she was planning such a trip."

Why did he suddenly break off with my daughter? Did he ever care for her or was that an imagined thing in her own fertile brain?

"It was quite a sudden thing for her, but she rushed things a bit, made her preparations, and got off in a whirl."

"That will be a pleasant thing for Betsy. I have never been to

Europe. Maybe when I return to Japan, I go way around." He laughed at his own attempt to express his thoughts.

"I hope you can, Dr. Tada. It will be a great experience for you."

After these pleasantries, Minoru was more at ease with his illustrious father. When he rose to leave, not wishing to encroach upon the great doctor's valuable time, he turned at the door to bow from the hips, "In your letters to Betsy, give her my yoroshiku (kind regards)." He then bowed himself away in true Japanese style.

While walking back to his room, Minoru noted that his knees were trembling. It was pure excitement in being near this father who did not know that he existed.

From that time, Minoru found himself seeking every opportunity to be near the man. Other students noting it, thought it an Oriental's innate desire to be near the one from whom they may learn the most. David McLean seemed as pleased by these encounters as was young Dr. Tada.

17

THE SUMMER BREAK for the medical students living at Miss Julia's came as a welcome respite from the gruelling days of study. Before the humid days of July had gone, their bags were packed and the places which they wished to visit were charted on the map across the great West. The bus company had arranged their itinerary, even to the stops for nights at the Y.M.C.A.'s along the route.

On the trip they saw much to make them wonder about the country in which they were studying. At the Grand Canyon, the place they all wanted most to see, they spent a week. There they encountered other students who had come to see the natural wonders of the West.

While Minoru clung to his little donkey, making the perilous descent into the mammoth gorge, watching his little beast step almost daintily on the steep path ahead of him, he could hear a woman's voice speaking in Japanese to her tiny mount. *"Dozo-kiwotsukete kudasai* (Please be careful.)"

When the caravan of long-legged humans astride little donkeys, finally arrived at the bottom of the gorge, Minoru went immediately to search for the one who had been pleading in his native tongue. He found her without delay, a trim graceful figure dressed in brown corduroy slacks and a shirt the color of autumn woods. Her jet-black hair hung in shining rolls to her shoulders topped by a jaunty straw hat which came to a saucy peak at the top. She was Japanese in appearance; American in actions. When Minoru spoke to her in Japanese, she whirled to look at the tall man with round expressive eyes standing beside her. She extended her hand in typical American friendliness and introduced herself.

"I am Matsuko Hara from Seattle, Washington. Where do you come from?"

When he introduced himself, she continued to talk.

"You must have heard my pleas to the little beast."

"I did, and wondered why you thought he could understand Japanese better than English." They laughed together.

"It was a vain hope that he might understand the tones *and* my fright, while my companions would not sense my panic. I was really frightened. Never again!"

After that meeting, Minoru saw to it that he viewed all the wonderful sights with Matsuko. Of all the magnificent wonders that he saw that week, nothing came near to the wonder of this Japanese-American girl. Several times he caught her shyly looking at him with a pleased gleam in her eyes. She evidently liked what she was seeing too.

When the time came for them to go their separate ways, Minoru caught both of her hands in his,

"This is not good-by, Matsuko. I am already making plans to carry you with me when I return to Japan next summer — say in September."

She blushed prettily and looked straight into his eyes to say, "I've always planned to make a trip to Japan someday!" She turned quickly away to join her group for the trip back to the west coast.

The early days of September found Minoru and Jon Cordez back in their places at Miss Julia's: the other men had separated from them at the Canyon and headed home across the Pacific, their American studies behind them.

Miss Julia's house seemed strangely empty to them, but she gave them the news that new students would be arriving during the week.

"This year," she told them, "the new ones come from Europe: two Germans, one Swede and one Swiss."

Minoru was anxious to have them arrive so they might get acquainted before the opening of work at the Center. The four Orientals had given him such a widened horizon of the Orient, he knew the Occidentals would open for him a wider vista of the world and a better understanding of its problems. He tried to express this to Miss Julia one day.

"We certainly get our views of the world widened by living here at your home, Miss Julia. Not only do we get our medical training but we get our windows of understanding thrown open to the world. This is a great thing you do for us, you know."

"Just think how much I do for myself, Minoru. Besides getting my windows of understanding thrown open wide, I now have *sons* all over the world. Someday, before I'm too old, I shall close shop here and set out to visit my sons — the sights of interest, of course, will be incidental: Scandinavia, Scotland, England, then through the Suez into the Red Sea, and to the Orient — around the world!"

"Make Japan your last stop and stay in my home for a long visit. Most people want to see Japan in spring, but really fall is the choice season. The leaves are beautiful then and the rains are not much. I like the fall best of the seasons."

For the first time Minoru spoke to her of his home, of Obasan who looked after things in his absence.

Questions about his family trembled on Miss Julia's lips, but she did not ask them. There were many things about this young man which had intrigued her from the beginning. He certainly was different, not only in appearance but in his ways of doing things. At all times he was impeccably dressed. He never squandered his money as her rich "boys" invariably did; neither was he penurious as the poor guests were forced to be. He had never mentioned his family nor had he ever shown her pictures as the others did after they began to accept her as a friend rather than a landlady.

The day the new guests arrived, Minoru was assigned to meet the Swede, Nels Christenson. He was easily spotted at the station and his English was sufficiently clear. They understood each other at once.

That night, according to Miss Julia's custom, the new men were her guests at dinner. Minoru had his first experience of serving a table. As he passed the plates he smiled to think what Obasan would say if she could see him in the role of waiter.

He watched Miss Julia at the head of the table making these men feel her warm interest in each one of them — strangers in a strange land.

He wondered at the fondness with which he regarded his *Aunt*. Often in his imagination he played at saying to her abruptly some-day, "You are really my aunt, Miss Julia. It would be natural for you to spend a long time in my home in Japan."

While on his trip West, Minoru often wondered if Dr. McLean were getting a break from his busy round. If so, what he was doing with it? Now that he was back at the Center, he was anxious to see the chief of surgeons before the academic grind was set in motion again. He decided to drop by his private office to speak to him, but, once there, standing outside the door, his nerve almost gave way. His hand shook as he raised it to tap on the door.

When the doctor heard the knock, he called out a hearty welcome, and, the moment David McLean saw who was standing in his door, he stood to reach his hand across the desk in welcome. This was the first time Minoru had felt the father's touch upon his hand. An unbelievable thrill raced through his being as he held the doctor's hand in his own. He looked down at the long fingers grasping his own, and, except for the color of the two hands, they were amazingly similar.

"How are you, Dr. Tada? How was the trip West?" Minoru felt the warmth of the greeting and was able to swallow the lump of excitement in his throat to answer, "Our bus trip was wonderful. For little money we saw much country."

For some reason this brought laughter from David McLean. "Out West one always sees much country. What did you enjoy most?"

"The Grand Canyon. It is not believed even after one sees it. Never have I seen such a sight!" *I also met my future bride,* he wanted to say.

After other exchanges, happenings of the summer, Minoru rose to leave. "I only stopped to say hello; I must not take up more of your valuable time." He bowed from the waist as he bade his father good-by. As he turned down the hall, he almost ran into Betsy who was on her way to her father's office. Both were visibly surprised.

"Have you been in my father's office?" she asked almost too sharply.

"Yes, for a moment — to greet him after summer. It seems such a long time since I saw him." This comment seemed a bit queer to Betsy who stored it away in her mind for future consideration.

"How was your trip to Europe?" Minoru asked as if really interested.

"Wonderful, better than ever before. I have been over three times, but I could go every summer and not see all that I want to see. This time we tried for new and not too frequented places. I think these out-of-the way places hold more charm than the beaten trail. How about your break?"

"Wonderful. I took many photographs. Someday I will show if you like." He drew out one lone picture and handed it to her. "I met her on the tour," he said happily.

Betsy took the picture in her hands and scanned it closely. A slender Japanese girl, looking stylish even in her hiking togs. "Why she's Japanese, isn't she?"

"Yes, it is so," Minoru laughed, "yet she is also American. She is a Nisei, second generation, we call them."

"Where did you meet her, Minoru?" Betsy was feigning more interest than she was feeling.

"At the bottom of the Grand Canyon. All of us rode donkeys down. She had never ridden one before. I had never ridden a donkey. Have you ever?"

"Yes, years ago when I was a small girl.

"She's very attractive, Minoru. Where does she live?"

"She lives in Seattle, Washington. Someday she hopes to come to Japan. She has never been there."

Betsy McLean abruptly handed back the picture, and went on her way. She was irked by the fact that Minoru seemed friendly enough to drop in to see her illustrious father. Few men ever won that intimacy; he was too Olympian for that. This proved her point. Her father *had* bribed this boy and ruined her cleverly laid plan.

She felt that the showing of the picture was Minoru's way of telling her that, when he did become interested in a girl, she would be from his part of the world — from his own people.

Well, he need not have bothered. Surely he never thought that I could become interested in him. Neither would he have ever fallen in love with me. I must admit it — for once in my life my fluttering eyelids went unseen — and were not fully understood.

No sooner had she entered her father's office and closed the door behind her than she said,

"I met your young Japanese 'protege' down the hall. Since when did you two get so clubby?" Her father laughed aloud.

"I think it was after you told me that you were in love with him. I took the only way I knew to find out what sort of a fellow he is, and what his intentions are."

"Did he reveal them to you?" she snapped.

"Not at all. I must confess that, except for the fact that he belongs to a different world from yours, he is my type of man. I can understand why you would be drawn to him, Baby. If you really want to let yourself fall in love with him, we can work things out for him to stay on this side of the world. He will be a valuable surgeon anywhere. Before he came to America, he had had one year of practicing surgery; but, since surgeons are so scarce in Japan, he had performed operations that American surgeons have to wait years to perform. He has kept abreast of all the new strides in surgery by reading medical journals in both German and English. He's a find."

"In other words, I have your blessings to marry a Japanese?" Betsy asked with a snarl in her voice which was frightening to her father.

"If Dr. Tada loves you and you love him, yes, you have my blessings."

Betsy turned pale with anger. She sat looking levelly at this man whom she had so misjudged. He had deliberately let her fall into her own "elephant's hole," dug so cunningly for him.

"Do you honestly think that I'd stoop to such a thing as marrying a Japanese? Don't you see that I was just using him to show you what weird things can happen when you dare tamper with another's life? I wanted to frighten you into letting me have my way where Bob Moreland is concerned. Now, are you satisfied?"

David McLean was speechless. He sat looking at his ruthless daughter and realized that he was partially responsible for her attitude. He and Martha had never really agreed on child rearing. For the most part, he had left Betsy to his wife who never saw any fault in their beautiful daughter. David realized, now that it was too late, that Betsy had not had enough spankings in her childhood. He felt that he'd like to give her a good one now. In spite of these thoughts, he was able to keep himself in perfect control, though he seethed inside.

"Well, because of you and your foolishness, I have been able to form a real friendship with a worthy young man. At least, I thank you for bringing him into my life."

It was after dinner that night that Betsy flatly told her father what was in her social plans for the winter season.

"Dad, I am dating Bob Moreland again and you might as well get used to the idea." She waited for him to speak, but he remained discreetly silent. "Well, aren't you mildly interested?" she asked hotly.

"Betsy, you are twenty-two, as you've reminded me several times lately. By this time you should know your own mind. It is your life; I am not capable of telling you how to conduct it. My opinion of Bob Moreland has not changed. This rekindling of the flame for him is your doing and I am sorry. You are going to get badly scorched, my child, but I cannot help you. Bob will never amount to a row of pins simply because he doesn't care about anything or anybody but himself. There can be no happiness with such a man, Betsy."

Here was a flare of anger which her father had never seen before in his daughter. Her cheeks were aflame with passion. "He *does* care about me — of that I am sure. It just may be that you are going to have to change some of your ideas about Bob." She flounced out of the room and up the stairs without turning back.

David McLean sat as one who has been hit over the head with a hammer. He had given the affair between his daughter and Bob Moreland not a single thought in months. He had not known that the thing had rekindled, but he knew defeat when he met it. His head began to ache and his stomach to grow queasy. He knew that *this* time he would not turn a hand to stop his child in her headlong plunge.

A strange thought flitted across his stunned mind. *After all, aren't that pair strangely alike: both thoroughly spoiled, thoroughly selfish, both know that there is plenty of money but know nothing of how it was earned? Come to think of it, they richly deserve each other.*

He continued to sit in his den until past midnight. He remembered reading years ago, Edgar Allen Poe's *The Fall of the House of Usher*. After all the family had died, the old house sank slowly into the lake. He felt that his own beautiful house was sinking; so much had depended on Betsy, his only child. So much had been invested in her. Something about it was all wrong, dead wrong. He was heartsick, crushed. Tomorrow was Sunday. He would call Julia, even at this late hour, to ask her to have dinner with him. He was in sore need of something — someone.

When he dialed her number, he could tell by her voice that she had been awakened from sleep and was a bit frightened.

"What on earth is it, David? Is anything the matter?"

"Much has happened, but I really called to ask you to have dinner with me tomorrow. Betsy has business elsewhere and I hate being alone."

On the other end of the line Julia hesitated as if she were impatient with him for calling, but when she answered, her voice was warm and loving. "Well, let's make a bargain, David. I'll come to dinner with you if you will get up early and go to church with me. How about it?"

It was his time to pause. *How long has it been since I have been in a church? Maybe this desperate situation calls for going to church again. It certainly calls for something! I should have thought of this before I called. Church is a must for Julia, nothing keeps her from it.*

"All right, Sis, it's a bargain, I'll meet you there and we'll come straight here from the service."

When he hung up, he sat wondering why he had been foolish enough to let Julia trap him into such a bargain.

That night as he slept, he was led in devious paths of frustration in his dreams. When he awoke, only one incident of the disturbed night lingered in his memory; he had been walking down a mountain path with thick jungle growth all about him. Betsy, still a small child, had been holding fast his hand. Suddenly, without warning, she broke his hold on her and disappeared into the jungle. He called loudly, called until his throat was raw. Then he had turned from his futile search to seek help in finding her. When he awoke his night clothes were drenched with perspiration and his heart was beating in his chest like a hammer.

18

THE NEXT MORNING while breakfasting alone, David McLean kept recalling the awful dream which had put him on a rack last night. He had never been one to put any credence in dreams, but even he could interpret this one. He was losing his daughter! If and when she threw her lot in with a character like Bob Moreland, she was entering a jungle for sure. As he lifted his coffee cup to his lips, he noticed a slight tremor in his hand.

Part of this nervousness, he knew, was caused by the idea of going to church with Julia. He sat drinking his coffee and mentally kicking himself for having made such a bargain. He'd simply let Julia slip up on his blind side, and no one else could do it with Julia's cleverness. He smiled, recalling the number of times she had done it in their childhood. One never knew that he was in her clutches until it was too late.

He tried to remember when it was that he had stopped attending church. In their youth, he and Julia were regular attendants at both Sunday school and church. His mother and father were pillars of old St. Mark's. Unless someone was very sick, the four of them were in their pew and on time.

He remembered after he and Martha were married — just before Betsy was born — they had had a long, frank discussion about church attendance. In her condition, Martha could not go, or felt that she couldn't, though she had not stopped attending other things. They had been at a party the night before Betsy came. He remembered that Martha's obstetrician was at the same party and whispered in his wife's ear, "At least we can keep an eye on each other, Martha. There could be no better arrangement than this."

After that frank discussion about church attendance, they had decided that it was foolish to keep up something simply because your parents thought that it was the thing to do.

"What do you really get out of attending church?" Martha had asked in her forthright way.

"I can't say that I have been too regular in attendance in the last few years, but when I do go, I come away with the sense of having rested. The music is always good, I think; the money spent on music at St. Mark's is well-spent; I have been known to catch a snooze during the sermon sometimes — that is restful." He smiled naughtily at his wife.

"*You* should have to tell me that!" Martha said, "I'm the one who feels duty bound to stay awake so that I can punch you before you work up to a snore. Do you ever get help from a sermon?"

"Nothing special. It isn't often that the minister says anything which makes me want to stand up and sing . . ."

"I should hope not," Martha burst out laughing. "Have you ever heard yourself sing?"

"Well, stop putting the screws on me, and tell me how you react to it," he remembered asking Martha.

"David, remember that I did not come from church-going folks. My parents could take it or leave it as the mood struck them — they mostly left it. Naturally I was left to make my own choice about it. When my little friends went, there I was, too, but, there came a time when most of us gave it up. It ceased to be a status symbol for us. Now that our baby is on its way, and I am staying at home, I admit that I am finding the quiet Sunday mornings at home to my liking."

Together they had decided that it was juvenile of people to keep jumping through the hoops of religion just because a hoop was held up to them; so they had ceased going to church.

At the time of Martha's death, David had felt a little hypocritical in calling a minister, who never knew Martha, to conduct her funeral. Of course, he had kept up a nominal contribution to the church; the church always seemed to be hard up, and it had meant so much to his parents. He justified his request to the minister on that score, and hoped no one else thought about it. How could anyone have a funeral in the United States without a minister?

Betsy, therefore, had had very little church in her experience. There was a period when she went because her little friends were going. When her interest waned, and she stopped going, no one had urged her to continue.

Maybe, David McLean was thinking as he dressed for church, *maybe if we had seen to it that she keep up church attendance, she might be a more reasonable, less headstrong girl.*

Julia and I had church training, and we surely learned a few things which helped us; but, I spent some mighty boring hours on that hard church pew.

It had seemed to David in his youth that ministers tried themselves to see how utterly boring they could be, just for the heck of it.

On the drive to church, he began conjecturing on what men, among his friends, would be there today. He knew that Dr. Townsend and Clyde Weatherford would be. They were officers — the hypocrites! They were no better than he, and he knew that he could not serve in a position as a church officer. He remembered that they had asked him to serve on the board too (as someone told him) in an effort to get him back into the habit of coming to church. He thanked his good sense for having declined the offer. After all, a vestryman still meant a man with some spiritual standing. His father had been a vestryman at St. Mark's and a good one at that, though he had left his Scottish Presbyterian Church to join with his wife.

Julia was waiting for him in the foyer of the church. Looking neither to the right nor to the left, David moved after her down the carpeted aisle and slid into the old familiar pew. Julia immediately knelt in prayer on the stool used by his mother. Seeing her there, he was suddenly overcome with memories of his childhood, sitting close beside his mother with his head nestled in the soft fur of her coat. He was suddenly a little boy again, nibbling the whiskers of the fox fur which his mother wore. The poor fox ended up with not a whisker before his mother noticed where they had gone. Another memory: holding out a bloody baby tooth which he had wiggled all the way to church, hoping to collect his quarter before they reached the pew. He had held it out in triumph to his mother as she read the morning prayer and watched the look of shock on her face. Remembering these things now, he chuckled to himself and wondered, *Why could not I have had a son? Little boys are such reminders of one's own boyhood. I would have loved a boy. Girls wind you about their fingers, but a son is more a part of a man.*

Julia rose from her knees with the light of spiritual repose on her face, as if she really had been speaking to God. David noticed and watched the lovely light filtering through the old stained glass windows, while the muted tones of the old organ filled the sanctuary.

When the service began, he reached for a prayerbook and found the proper place. As the rector read the words and the audience gave response, he found meaning here, not understood in his childhood, and truths which he had forgotten. As the responses rolled about him, "Lord, have mercy upon us," he let his eyes wander to faces of the worshipers about him, and wondered if any of them were really praying this from their hearts. He certainly needed to ask God to have mercy upon himself. He had a deep need this morning for God — not One, way off in the blue yonder where his childhood God had been, but One who could walk beside him and still his fears.

When they sang a hymn his thoughts of those about him were even worse. *Here folks are saying words set to music which they wouldn't be caught saying outright, but, when others are bellowing them out, it seems right for them to sing them, so they do.*

> How dear to me, O Lord of Hosts
> The place where thou dost dwell;
> The tabernacles of Thy grace
> In pleasantness excel.

The idea of anyone singing those words. He certainly was not going to be so immature!

He listened carefully to the sermon of the morning. He did this, not in any critical mood, but to find if there would be one word which would lift the burden carried in his heart; one word from scripture which would be relevant for a surgeon in dire need.

Platitudes delivered in sonorous tones, which seem to come from the minister's chest cavity, were all that he heard. David found himself thinking. *This fellow must have been an "A" student in voice at the seminary.* He felt chilled by the lack of a spiritual message instead of warmed, as he needed to be.

When the service was over, David McLean found himself surrounded by people anxious to shake his hand in greeting. Some were friends from boyhood days, some were those who knew him professionally, and were pleased that he had joined them at the church.

Somewhere in the sinful pocket of his mind, he wondered if some of them were not thinking of the contributions which he could make to the church rather than the pleasure of his company at the service.

His name was still on the church roll, he supposed; but, to most of those who spoke to him, he was a stranger known only because of his prominence in the medical profession.

Going out of the church, he deliberately stepped aside from shaking hands with the minister at the front door. He had no desire to speak to him and he certainly was not going to say that he thought the message good. It wasn't. He could say that it was well-delivered, but he had the idea that the rector was well aware of his ability in that area. As David McLean was thinking this, he wormed his way around the crowd and reached the outside to wait for Julia.

On the way home, Julia asked him, "How did you enjoy the service, David?"

"Maybe a church service is not meant to be enjoyed, Julia. I neither enjoyed it nor was I helped by it. Honestly, I went there today needing and seeking help, Sis, the first bit of spiritual hunger I ever experienced in my life, and what did I get? Moonlight and Roses — poor quality of those!"

David's tone was bitter, and Julia, a wise woman, remained silent. She would neither try to defend the service nor the minister simply because she was a loyal church-goer. Maybe this brother of hers was trying to say something which would be worth her while to hear.

"Where was the service lacking, David?" she asked gently.

"You tell me, Julia. You are versed in such things. I'm a greenhorn, but honestly, except for those wonderful rolling tones, there was not much to it. How could anyone be helped by knowing that the whole of Christendom is moving closer together, and 'All peoples of the world' are drawing together in a fuzzy warmth of the Christian community'? From what he implied, anyone who comes to church will be warmed by a fellowship. That's not true. I can get fellowship — warmer than that — at my club. I feel warmed and wanted there — and accepted. There are Catholics there, and Jews as well as several different nationalities — we are all professional men and have a common interest; therefore, we feel at one with each other. That is not Christian fellowship — there is nothing Christian about it, just as there will be little Christian about what he is talking about. It's wacky — that's what!

"Another thing, Julia, that man's so-called sermon could be delivered in any gathering, anywhere without causing a ripple of dissension. Have messages in the churches shrunk to that drivel? I feel very fortunate that I have been able to escape them during these past years."

He waited for his sister to speak. She did after a bit of thinking first.

"It has been a long time since we have discussed anything of a religious nature, David. I have kept on being a regular attendant at church even though I have felt the central Christian message being watered down — even by-passed. I have wanted to discuss them with you; but, knowing your attitude, I knew that it would drive you further away from the church than you already are.

"At church the sermon is not the main thing with me. I worship God there — in His house, through prayers and hymns. In fact, the present rector touches scripture only when he feels that he must prove a point by it. I like Dr. Hendrickson personally, but I do confess that his messages leave me cold. This I have kept to myself, for he is a popular rector, and I'd be the last person on earth to speak a word of criticism against him."

"That is where you and I differ, Sis. Who was it who said, 'The best way to let the world go to the dogs is to let all good people say nothing.' You typify that group, Julia, but I belong to those who feel that it is all a waste of time and so stay at home. Which of us is more guilty?"

"Now, David, be fair. You and Martha stopped attending church long before Dr. Hendrickson came to us. You really belong to those who never really believed what the church teaches, therefore it seems hypocritical to you to keep up pretenses. In a way you are mentally honest. On the other hand, you never studied or tried to find God through Christ.

"I still get my greatest inspiration from reading the Bible and I keep going to God's House to meet with many who feel as I do. From the liturgy of the church I get renewed strength on Sunday mornings that I get nowhere else.

"I used to encourage the boys in my home to attend church with me. Some of them go with me occasionally; some not at all. I always ask them at least once; most of them accept. Those who know nothing of Christianity look upon that one experience as another strange thing in a strange land; some look upon it as an excellent way to hear good English spoken. But, now that Dr. Hendrickson is there, I do not even ask them the once. I do urge them to go to other churches where they will hear a gospel message. I know they will get nothing from our services.

"I had a most interesting experience this year with Minoru Tada. He went with me only once. He said little about it except that he was so busy listening to the tune of Dr. Hendrickson's English, he caught nothing of his words."

"He's an interesting chap. I am sorry that Betsy stopped seeing him," her brother said.

"David McLean, you can't really mean it." His sister was shocked.

"It may shock you, Julia, but I do truly mean it."

"Betsy intimated to me that it was you, David, who broke them up, that was after she quizzed me about my part in doing it."

"Well, that's news! To me she said flatly the other day, that she was using the young Japanese to shock me so that I'd blow my top, and would consent to her seeing Bob Moreland again. She is dating him again, Sis, and there is not a thing that I can do about it. She is twenty-two years old; I'm going to hands-off."

"Is that what is troubling you, David? I hadn't dreamed that Betsy could be so ruthless as to play with the affections of young Dr. Tada. Fact of the matter is, David, I think she was infuriated that she could not get to first base with him. Minoru terminated their relationship himself, I know, because I heard them talking on the 'phone."

They got out of the car and went into the house. At dinner, David looked up suddenly to say,

"It's strange, Julia, that you could have swallowed all that minister said about the 'warm one-ness among the peoples of the world,' and yet are shocked over the idea of your niece falling in love with a man like Minoru Tada."

19

ON AN AFTERNOON in late October, when the trees were beginning to lose their autumnal glory and there was a decided chill in the air, to still the restlessness within him, Minoru scheduled his work so that he might have an uninterrupted evening in the dissecting laboratory. Many questions in his ever-seeking mind were yet unanswered, even after observing the operations and hearing the lectures which followed them.

When he entered the dark, still laboratory he immediately flooded the place with light. Going immediately to his table, he removed the cover from the female cadaver. As he settled down to work he was remembering the first harrowing days in Kyoto when such a sight as this almost wrecked his medical career. He knew, even now, that he had not come to terms with the mystery of death. He now accepted the fact of it and worked to *save* life.

As he traced the blood vessels down the young cadaver's arm, the physical solutions to his problems seemed no longer important; something larger was claiming his thoughts tonight. He held the woman's arm in his hand and looked searchingly at it. The marvelous mechanism of the intricately laced tendons, muscles, flesh, nerves and blood vessels were woven not only for strength but for grace and beauty as well. "Who is the designer of such a thing?" he suddenly heard his voice asking the empty room. As the question, which crowded his mind was spoken aloud, Minoru knew! There was a presence in the room. It filled him and it filled the laboratory. He instinctively knew that something divine, holy and permanent had happened to him. He knew also that life would never be the same. Suddenly he seemed to be lifted to a new level of consciousness — a new dimension of the senses.

Far away he seemed to hear Mrs. Grady's voice speaking of God's revelation through Jesus Christ, His messenger to the world. He thought of Matsuko as they had stood watching the beauty of twilight fall like a multi-colored curtain across the shadow-filled canyon, asking him, "Minoru, you believe in God, don't you?"

"No I don't," he had answered honestly, "though at such a time as this, in the face of such overwhelming beauty, I feel that some intelligence must be back of it."

"My family are Christians," Matsuko told him simply. "Our God is ever with us, ever near."

At this moment God is near me too, Matsuko, he was saying in his mind. *He is Creator, Sustainer and Ruler of the universe. I know it for I have just stumbled across irrefutable proof. For me, this is enough!*

Another thing he knew: he would never be able to approach a patient lying in anesthetized sleep waiting for his surgeon's knife, without first stopping to connect himself to this almighty Power of the Creator.

The glory of this moment Minoru was never to lose. He sat quietly holding the feminine arm in his hand letting the elation of this magic moment sink deep into his consciousness.

Then, as if walking upon holy ground he tip-toed about the room restoring order, turned out the lights and started toward Miss Julia's, walking under the star-studded sky. Once in his room he went straight to his desk and began to try to record this overpowering experience in a letter to Matsuko.

> I need help at this point. I long to talk this over with someone who can direct my next steps; who can guide me in this new light and life.

When the letter was sealed, he left his room to post it in the box up the street. Once out in the open, he decided to wander about before going back to his room. There was too much joy, too much wonder in his soul to think of getting to bed. Slowly along the tree-lined street he walked, looking up at the stars pricking through the velvety blackness of the sky, watchful eyes from eternity. For the first time he experienced the thrill of realizing that he was a tiny speck of God's great universe.

Though he was unversed in giving praise to The Almighty, he did so now, improvising in his native tongue, joining with all creation in declaring the Glory of God.

Once back in his room, he took the Bible, which he had found in his drawer, and turned to John's Gospel.

> In the beginning was the Word, and the Word was with God, and the Word was God. He was in the beginning with God; all things were made by him and without him was not anything made that was made. In him was life, and the life was the light of men. The light shines in darkness and the darkness has not overcome it.

That light which came into the world still shines. I know Christ is indeed the Light — and the Word — both have entered my heart.

Early in November when Minoru returned home from a day at the Center he found two letters waiting for him. He opened Matsuko's first:

> If you have no better plans for your Christmas holidays, my parents suggest that you might like to spend them in a Japanese home where you can enjoy Japanese food again, as well as give them a chance to know you for themselves rather than second hand through their daughter. Of course, I want to see you again, too. Letters are poor substitutes for personal encounters. Please try to join us.

> There is much doing in our Japanese community during the holidays, much of the activity is centered in Old World celebrations which you may enjoy. Our family is Christian, as I told you last summer, so we find ourselves having double celebrations; it makes for a happy time. All of us want you to be with us. The daughter of the house would be especially happy to have you. Let us know if you can make it — and when.

After finishing the letter, his mind began to leap ahead to a Christmas — his first as a Christian — with the girl whom he already knew was destined to be his wife, and with her family which might someday be his own also. This would be the perfect substitute for a return to Takarazuka, even better, since he would be with Matsuko.

He picked up the other letter and was surprised to see that it was from Louisville, Kentucky, yet it was from Toshio. *How in the world can this be?* he was thinking as he tore into the envelope.

> Minoru, this will be a shock for you, I know. I am also in America for a year of study, in the theological seminary on scholarship given by the American Mission Board. I have finished my seminary training in Japan; this is a bonus — a surprise gift which I never expected.

> I know that I should have written you before this. Your letter, telling of your wonderful experience, was sent back from Japan to me here. I must see you for a long talk. If you have free time at Christmas why not spend it with me here? We are not too far apart as the train runs.

> I need not comment on my struggles of trying to get along on my meager English. You know so well what it means, however, everyone is being most kind to me, even the professors speak deliberately and slowly for my sake. I do make progress. Let me hear right away if you can be with me.

> Always your friend,
> Toshio.

Having these two letters arrive on the same mail had a special meaning for Minoru. He drew from his desk the maps collected on the summer tours, and began to study distances. He knew, as he did so, no distance could keep him from visiting these two places. He would go first to Toshio for a day or two, then fly to Seattle to save as much time as possible. Feeling like a school boy with an unexpected gift in his pocket, he worked out the schedules and sent letters accepting both invitations, noting the days he could spend at each place.

His bags were packed before the final take-off. As soon as the last lecture was over, he rode all the miles to the station in a taxi just to get the feel of traveling excitement. Once on the train, the enveloping warmth, the soft comfort of the seat and the rhythmic thumping of the turning wheels beneath him, lulled him to sleep. When he awoke darkness had fallen; he had missed the interesting scenery along the way.

When the train pulled into the dimly lit terminal at Louisville, Toshio was on the platform to greet him. Minoru felt like a child being met by a parent. Instinctively, the two Japanese men, when face to face with one another, even in the midst of the hurrying American crowd, began bowing in true Japanese fashion. Suddenly realizing that they were making a spectacle of themselves, they hurriedly shook hands and burst into laughter.

In the comfortable Seminary quarters, Toshio introduced his friend to fellow students who came in and out as they hurried to catch trains and planes for distant homes. The next day all the excitement had died down; the halls were deserted save for the two Japanese friends. Minoru had been given permission to share the dormitory room with Toshio for their days together.

They liked the exquisite quiet of the place and the time to catch up on the happenings since they last met. Minoru wanted to know every step which had brought his friend to America. Toshio wanted to know all that had happened at the medical center during the first year of study and what the future promised his friend.

"You're not thinking of staying in America, are you, Minoru? After learning the princely salaries American doctors demand, I thought you might be ready to cash in on the American part of you, and swing into a new orbit," Toshio told him jokingly.

"I've never given that a thought. It's back home for me. More and more I am conscious of how far behind Japan is in the science of medicine. I want to get back to help all I can. When I return, Toshio, I think I shall be taking a wife with me, at least this is my plan. When I leave you, I'm flying to Seattle to see if it may not come to pass."

x

"An American wife!" Toshio almost shouted the question, remembering all that Minoru had said about Mrs. Grady.

"An American, yes, but also a Japanese — a Nisei." He told him then about Matsuko and all that he knew of her family. "Wish me success," he added.

"I do, Minoru. I think that's the best news you've told me yet."

"My letter telling you of my wonderful experience in the dissecting laboratory reached you, you told me in the letter."

"Yes, it was sent back to me here and I am so anxious to hear all about it. However, tomorrow night we are to be dinner guests at the Seminary President's home. I want him to hear it too, and I want to hear what he has to give you in the way of directions for your spiritual development."

Through all the exchange of happenings, not once did Minoru mention to his friend that he was studying at the Center where his illustrious father was chief of surgeons. Somehow that was one secret he wished to share with no one. There was something too wonderful about it, too deep and sacred.

Both Toshio and Minoru had read stories about dinners in American homes at Christmas time, but the actual experience with the Lewis family was more vivid than they had imagined. Dr. Lewis was the perfect host, but at his own table, he was no longer the exalted Sensei (teacher), he was just "Dad" to his sons and daughter, taking their ribbings with a familiarity not known to Orientals. Dr. Lewis took all his children gave him in high good humor, encouraged his wife to take sides with him as their children pitted their wits against their parents'. It was a losing game for the two of them; these children, to whom they had given so much freedom of expression, were a bit too agile for them. Such an exchange over the dinner table was a new and delightful experience for the two Japanese. They watched and listened with sparkling interest.

When dinner was over, and the young people scattered to their activities, the three men withdrew into the den where Mrs. Lewis soon joined them. There Toshio asked Minoru to relate to them the astounding revelation of God which came to him in the dissecting laboratory, given at a time when Minoru felt great need in so many areas of his life.

Minoru told of the experience which had completely changed the course of his life; told it simply, describing the glory of the moment when clogging, conflicting currents of his life seemed to have been drained from him, and a peace that he had never experienced flowed into the void.

When he had finished, Dr. Lewis sat a long moment without speaking. Clearing his throat of the lump of emotion, he said, "Thank you for sharing this with us, Dr. Tada. It is a story that I shall never forget, and probably will use many times. Christians — others too, but especially Christians — need to be reminded that God's love is a giant beam constantly sweeping across the world. Those who are brought face to face with Him in Christ, His Son, know the truth that sets them free. Your experience is certainly unique. I can't recall ever hearing of a modern revelation just like this."

With this as a starting point, questions and answers were exchanged among the four of them. Many problems concerning the Christian way of life were passed on to the newest member of "The Way."

The trip from Louisville to Seattle was, as Toshio said it would be, "a zip-trip." Minoru had been on Japanese planes before but this was his first experience on a jet. It seemed to him the plane bounded from the ground, high into the cotton wool clouds, and there it seemed to hang motionless.

In Seattle he found himself in a thoroughly Americanized home peopled with Japanese. This took a bit of adjusting on his part. Matsuko was even lovelier than he had remembered her, more glowing and charming. The parents spoke to him only in Japanese from their first greeting. It was as if they were hungry to use again the language of their childhood. Matsuko's brother was so Americanized one could tell that he was Japanese only by looking at him. When Minoru commented on the fact, Randy Hara heard and turned quickly to say, "I'm not Japanese, I'm an American."

"He is right, of course," Mrs. Hara said, "and he will never be anything else.

"We made him that when we let him be born in this country. He has no desire to go to Japan."

After Minoru was in bed that night, in a room shared with Randy sleeping the sound sleep of a sixteen-year-old, he lay thinking of the strange turns in life which affect those who are given no choice in the matter. There was Randy not realizing that he belonged to the Japanese race; here was Minoru Tada belonging to both sides of the world, yet feeling only Japanese.

Just before sleep overtook him, Minoru thought fleetingly of what it would mean to Matsuko to throw her loyalties to a land she had never seen but to which she belonged by blood. Tomorrow he planned to ask her to be his wife.

Minoru expressed a desire to walk in the beautiful park which he had seen in passing, near the Hara home, and as they walked along in the crisp air of the late December day, he carried out his resolve.

"Matsuko, I cannot make love to you in the true American way, but as I have told you over and over in my letters, I truly do love you. You are the only girl I have ever seen with whom I want to spend the rest of my life; you are the only one who can make my lonely life complete. I want to take you home to Japan with me as my wife. I don't want you to give me your answer now. Think it over and be prepared to answer before I return to school. With your permission, I'd like to discuss it with your parents. I want to tell them what sort of life you might expect as my wife in Japan."

Matsuko, with her cheeks and eyes aflame, looked up at this tall young man. Though he had proposed to her in a typical Japanese way, she knew that his love was deep and true; she knew that it would grow with the years. The thought which he bade her entertain was not entirely new to her.

"Minoru, you know this idea of going back with you to Japan will take some weighing. I can't decide it on the spur of the moment. You know that I'd never have let the folks invite you here, if I had not been more than mildly interested in you.

"Suppose we wait until we can discuss this with my parents. I am Japanese enough to respect their ideas about things. Their experience and wisdom should be considered in so great a step for their daughter."

The talk that night lasted a long time. In true Japanese fashion, the parents were unhurried about this important matter.

Minoru told them about his home in Takarazuka which Obasan kept for him in his absence. He spoke of his financial status and his ambition to build a small private hospital in the city of his birth. How well Matsuko's nurse's training would fit in with his scheme of things.

"You remember that in Japan the educated girls will not enter the nursing profession because they consider it menial work. Matsuko can help us to change that idea, and for the advancement of medicine it is necessary. Until we can improve nursing in Japan, we will make little progress."

Minoru did not wait for them to ask about his parents; he told them all, omitting only the fact that he knew that his father was an American doctor. He preferred to keep his identity hidden even from Matsuko until she became his wife.

The parents listened in silence to all that he had to tell them. When he had finished, Mr. Hara spoke.

"We feel that no one should be judged harshly for having been born out of wedlock. Such a person should be judged by what he makes of his life. In that area, you seem to be doing all right, Minoru.

"Right now, we cannot tell you how we feel about your taking our only daughter back to Japan with you. We do not know how Matsuko feels about it."

They all turned then to look at the daughter of the house to find her answer written in happiness across her face.

That night, when they were alone, Minoru found that making love in the American way was both easy and natural, when the most wonderful girl in all the world was in his arms.

On the last afternoon of the year, Minoru boarded his plane for the trip back to Cleveland. He did not notice the planes bounding from the ground nor the floating clouds, for he was mentally already in the clouds; he was in love for the first time in his life and his mind was filled with happiness and peace.

When the taxi let him out before Miss Julia's house, he let himself in with his own key, mounted the stairs to his room, ready and anxious to have the intervening months of the New Year to hurry past. Nothing would seem difficult to him now, with Matsuko waiting to become his bride.

20

ON NEW YEAR'S EVE David McLean sat by a fire in his den, running over in his mind the happenings of the last two weeks. He could not remember another time just like it; he hoped there would never be another. From the day that Betsy had declared her intentions to go her own way, things had gone awry. Nothing that he had suggested for the holidays were to her liking. He had suggested the two pre-Christmas symphonies which she had always enjoyed and loved; had tried to lay plans for a Christmas dinner with Julia and her two friends who for years had come to them on Christmas Day. Betsy had wanted none of it.

"Dad, how about going on with your affairs this year, and letting me go on with mine? I have so many engagements to which I am already committed. After all, Bob is running my schedule, and you can imagine how full it is going to be," she told him.

David McLean had looked at his daughter for a long moment before he spoke. He had never seen her so hard or so defiant. Knowing at that moment that his displeasure was the thing she wanted most, he decided not to cross her in any way. He would not give her that satisfaction.

"If that is the way you want it, Betsy, then that's the way we'll have it. Julia and I will make our plans. We'll be delighted to have the pleasure of your company any time you wish to give it. May I ask if you are planning to have Christmas dinner with us?"

He saw her attitude noticeably soften as he kept his voice low and unruffled.

"Bob said something about having dinner out at his place on Christmas Day. I haven't decided to do it yet. Would you mind very much if I did?"

"Yes, I'm afraid I would mind, Betsy, very much. Why don't you ask him to join us here for Christmas dinner?"

"Dad, after all the awful things you said *about* him, *to* him, two years ago! Do you think that he has forgotten? I wouldn't *think* of asking him here."

"Does that mean then, that our ways are to take opposite directions simply because I spoke the truth." There was an icy edge to her father's tone, entirely new to Betsy.

"We'll just have to wait to see about that. As things stand now, Bob is very touchy where you are concerned and I can understand why he would be."

"Listen, my child, are you really serious about this man after all the things which I have been forced, as a father, to put before you?" He waited for her to answer, but it was slow in coming; when it did come there was finality to her words.

"You might as well know it now as later, Dad, I am going to marry Bob Moreland before the new year gets far on its way. We have not set the date, but it will be in January. Since we know that you want none of this, we are not planning a wedding. We'll manage, possibly, at a Justice of the peace."

"No, Betsy, not that! Your mother always planned for you to have a church wedding. She even bought your veil in Brussels, remember? You were only fourteen years old at the time. I want you to have the wedding that your mother planned. I don't want you married in a courthouse; I'd like it to be in the church as Martha always pictured it. Talk it over with Bob, and then we'll talk some more."

David McLean saw a sardonic smirk flit around his daughter's lovely mouth.

"So, you want our wedding in the church! Doesn't it ever strike you a bit queer that you turn to the church for things like weddings and funerals when you ignore it most of the time?"

"Now wait a minute, young lady," David McLean said hotly, "I never have been exactly stingy when the hat was passed. I have paid enough into the church to be able to ask that my daughter's wedding be there. Don't think I have any qualms on that score. If you want a church wedding, you certainly are entitled to it at St. Marks."

As Betsy turned to go, she said over her shoulder, "We'll think about it and let you know. Remember that both Bob and I are strangers to the church and might not feel at home there. Then, too, we might be too honest to sail under false colors. We'll see."

What in the world did she mean by being too honest? If that couple are too honest about anything, that's something to talk about!

On Christmas Eve David McLean had been alone and restless. He reached for the newspaper to see if by chance any church in the city was having a service. He knew that none of the uptown churches would be having one. They got these things out of the way so as not to interfere with the social gatherings. Since Martha's death he had no longer gone to parties where folks drank too much and acted silly; he was still invited, but no one seemed offended that he never went. Being a doctor gave him the "out" he needed.

His eye fell upon a notice of a Christmas pageant, to be given at a small church on the edge of town. On sudden impulse he decided to go. No one there would know him. He would time his arrival so that he could slip into a back pew without being seen by anyone. Perhaps he could recapture some of the wonder he used to feel as he took part in the Christmas pageant.

From his home on the hill, he judged that it would take an hour to reach the little church. He timed his arrival exactly right, for already the lights had been extinguished, and there was only the light of candles over the hushed sanctuary when David McLean managed to find a seat on the back pew next to the aisle.

For a moment he felt silly over this thing he had done. He looked surreptitiously around him at those who sat near. The couple next to him were well over the hump of life and into old age. He could almost feel them remembering when their children had taken parts in this same story. Perhaps there were grandchildren for them to watch tonight.

Before the pageant began, Christmas carols were sung with rousing enthusiasm. These people did not hesitate to take out all vocal stops and let the welkin ring. There was no money spent here on hired singers — they made the joyful noise themselves and invited all others to share their freedom. David found himself singing with an abandon he had never thought possible. Things began to swing into focus; he found himself dredging up memories of his own boyhood as the second chapter of Luke's gospel began to unfold according to someone's idea of how things were on that Judean hill two thousand years ago. Somewhere deep inside him, there were pools of nostalgic sadness. To the very end he sat watching the wonderful story reach the climax: when the startled shepherds heard the angels' songs and the message of God to them as they were watching their sheep. Then they hastened to the manger "to see this thing, which has come to pass."

David found himself strangely moved by the memories which the manger scene brought back to him. When the curtains closed upon Mary, Joseph and the shepherds looking hopefully at the light emanating from the straw in the manger, David McLean slipped out and walked in darkness to his parked car. As he drove away another joyful carol was being sounded out into the cold frosty night.

Steering his car along the dimly lit streets, he had a feeling of having made a quick transition from manhood to boyhood. He found himself humming, "While Shepherds Watched Their Flocks by Night," and, to his surprise found the words coming back to him.

On this New Year's Eve, David had accepted an invitation to dinner with a member of his staff, who had invited a dozen other people to see the Old Year out with them. After dinner, David decided not to stay until midnight. He was never one who felt it necessary to see the Old Year out, or to ring the New Year in. These friends were accustomed to David's independent ways and were not surprised that he did not stay with them.

When he reached his silent house and let himself in, he flung his overcoat over the chair nearest the door and went into the den. Simply because he did not want his own thoughts tonight, he turned on the T.V. A New Year's celebration was going on. It all looked like rather strenuous fun to *him;* he turned it off.

He wondered if he were feeling his age more than folks said that he showed it; he sat wondering about many things: what the New Year would be for him with Betsy married, what her life would be with a man like Bob Moreland. He wondered if he should try to persuade Julia to sell the old house and come to live with him. He cancelled that idea with the realization of what Julia's life would be without the interest of her foreign students. The thought of her young men brought to his mind young Minoru Tada, a young doctor to be reckoned with. *Why couldn't I have a son like him? If I had married Michiko Takahashi we might have had one very much like him.* As soon as this thought brushed his mind, he smiled a wan smile and was thankful that such random thoughts did not need to be recorded. If it were so, the world would be thrown into such confusion there would be no unsnarling it.

David, deep in these memories, seemed to hear bells ringing a far off. He supposed that he was seeing the Old Year out in spite of himself. He glanced at the clock to see that it was already three o'clock in the morning. He sat bolt upright. The telephone was ringing with frightening insistency.

When he took up the receiver, he heard Carl Bond's voice, "David, this is Carl. There's been a wreck — your daughter Betsy and her escort. They've been brought here to the hospital. You'd better get here as soon as possible." David tried to speak but no sound would come. "David, are you all right?"

"Yes, I'm all right. How bad is it, Carl?"

"Very bad, David." With that, he hung up as if he did not wish to say more.

Feeling as if the roof had caved in upon him, David McLean turned to the stairs and began to mount them. He found that it was necessary to hold to the rail as he climbed. Once in his room he looked about uncertainly. For a moment he could not remember why he came. His overcoat was downstairs where he had flung it; it was fortunate that he did not need to dress. On his way down the stairs he had to catch himself on the railing to keep from pitching headlong to the bottom.

Somehow he managed to steer his car through the city to the hospital. The midnight traffic had cleared and he had the streets almost to himself. At the hospital he went immediately to find Carl Bond. He found him taking off his gown after returning from surgery.

The moment Dr. Bond looked up and saw David standing in the door, his face crumpled with sympathy. "David, Betsy was dead when they brought her in here. Bob Moreland, with his veins full of alcohol, has just died on the table."

David's legs would no longer sustain his weight. He sank into a nearby chair with his head in his hands. Now he understood how it felt to be on the receiving end of the line instead of the giving end. It was usually he who came to the loved ones waiting to know how the scales had tipped on the operating table. Here was his friend beside him trying to soften the blow for him. No hope could be held out to him. Death is final, and he, David McLean, would somehow have to accept it for his Betsy.

He remained so still in the miserable huddle into which he had fallen, Dr. Bond came to put an arm about his shoulder.

"She didn't have a chance, David. The car left the road on a curve and smashed into a tree on her side of the car. Bob Moreland's neck was broken. He lived only long enough to be brought here. I'm sorry, David. It's just one of those blinding things."

When David McLean spoke, his voice was more calm than his friend's had been, "Bob Moreland was drunk?" he asked.

"Bob Moreland had been drinking. No tests have been made."

"How about Betsy?" he asked in a voice watered with tears.

Dr. Bond was shocked at such a question from a father, but, since it had been asked, it deserved a truthful answer.

"Betsy had also been drinking. Come with me, David, I'm going to give you something to make you rest awhile. Do you want to see Betsy now?"

"Not now, Carl, a bit later. Will you make all the arrangements for me? One other thing, please tell the hall nurse to call my sister, Mrs. Kenneth Wentworth. Just have her say that I'd like her to meet me at my home around six o'clock." He looked at his watch and found that it was already five.

"Carl, I think I'd rather go straight home. Do you suppose you could find an aide around here who would drive my car? I dare not trust myself. Another thing, tell the nurse to say nothing about the accident to my sister. She will go to pieces. I'd prefer to tell her. She will know that something is wrong to be called this early in the morning. Thank you."

When the aide, who had finally been rounded up, drove the car up the long driveway of the house, they noticed that Julia's car was there before them. She and Dr. Minoru Tada were standing inside the door to meet him when he entered on the arm of the aide. Before Miss Julia could ask the question, he was blurting out the answer to them.

"Betsy and Bob Moreland were killed in a car wreck tonight. Betsy died at once — Bob died on the operating table."

Miss Julia collapsed in a chair as she heard the heart-breaking sob from her brother. Dr. Tada and the aide got them both upstairs and into beds. When they had yielded to sedation, the streaks of dawn were shooting long streamers into the gray morning sky. The New Year was checking in for its first day's run.

When Mrs. Hayes arrived and heard the news, she was also visibly shocked, but knowing what was expected of her, went immediately to the kitchen and busied herself getting breakfast for the two strange men, and plenty of coffee for them and herself.

While the aide sat in a chair idly flipping through a magazine, Minoru walked through the spacious rooms of his father's home, looking about without seeing. He too was stunned by the shocking news.

Betsy, Betsy, my sister and my friend, seemed a sobbing refrain in his mind. *How can things happen so suddenly? How can I believe that one so vital and beautiful as Betsy has had her life snuffed out like a candle's light?* Minoru felt himself crying inside.

By nine o'clock, the rooms downstairs were fast filling with friends who had heard the news over the early morning broadcast, and had hurried through breakfast to come immediately to offer their help and sympathy.

Minoru and the aide caught the first ride possible back to the city. They had done all they could in this sad situation — intimate friends were there to take over.

21

AFTER THE TRAGEDY in the McLean household, Minoru wandered about the house at Miss Julia's, wanting to be with his father yet fearing to presume too much. He kept hoping that Miss Julia would return and put him in direct contact again. Instead she sent a friend to collect the needed items to be brought to her at the McLean home.

In the privacy of his room Minoru read the newspaper account of the accident and wept for the two young lives snuffed out so abruptly. He read the plans for Betsy's funeral and felt that, in this awkward situation, he should carry his heartache in silence and alone.

Four days after the funeral he found Miss Julia at home, seated in her accustomed place by the window working needlepoint. She called to him as he entered the front door.

"Come in here, Minoru, if you have a moment to spare."

Minoru went into the room to welcome her home. "It is good to have you back, Miss Julia. We have all felt that our mother was away; that is not a good feeling."

Miss Julia smiled. He could tell that she was pleased with what he had said. "Thank you, Minoru. It's good to be home again, but for the next few weeks I shall be over at David's more than I shall be here with you all."

"How is Dr. McLean?" Minoru asked.

"I honestly don't know what to tell you. I think that he is still in a state of shock. Probably his worst time is yet to come, for he has not fully realized what has happened but realization is bound to come and I fear for him then."

"Why do you 'fear for him'?" Minoru wanted to know.

"Minoru, my brother is not a Christian so he is without hope in the face of this. He and his wife did nothing to encourage Betsy to a religious faith of her own. So far as I know, Betsy had no faith at all." Miss Julia began to cry softly in her handkerchief.

"My brother is wild with remorse. It seems that one of the last things Betsy said to him was a rebuke for his hypocrisy in religious matters. She seems to have inferred that folks, like my brother, who make a gesture toward Christianity are not as honest as those, like herself, who had rejected it altogether. Is that too complicated for you?" Miss Julia asked Minoru whose brow was puckered in perplexity. He seemed lost in the maze of her words.

"Yes, I fear so. I understand a little, but what means 'gesture toward Christianity'?"

As simply as she could, she explained how it is possible for a person to hold to the empty forms of Christian practices and yet understand nothing of its true meaning for their personal life. When she had finished, Minoru sat nodding his head in understanding.

"It is like the lamp and the electric light, is it not? Until the lamp is plugged into the current-power — it cannot be a light. Those who never really contact God remain cold lamps — just humans."

Miss Julia looked quickly at this amazing Oriental. Never had she heard a Christian truth expressed more succinctly by anyone. "Minoru, my brother told me to thank you for your help the morning you went to his home with me. He speaks so highly of you as a man, as well as a doctor. Someday soon you must go with me to see him."

Minoru, flushed with pleasure, asked, "Will he be able to start with us at the Center?"

"I doubt it. In fact it wouldn't surprise me if it were weeks before he will resume his duties. That's my idea; I could be wrong and I hope that I am. He *could* feel that work is his best panacea at this point. So, let's just hope and wait to see."

Each day at the Center, Minoru made a point to walk past the surgeon's private office, hoping for a glimpse of him. He found he was never able to work up the nerve to ask the secretary or to tap upon the door to see if the familiar voice would bid him enter.

In late February, Minoru caught a glimpse of his father entering the building. His heart bounded with delight; his pulse beat rapidly. He had an impulse to run across the campus to greet him. He stifled the impulse and waited to see if the surgeon would attempt to meet his scheduled lecture that afternoon. There, he could see for himself how things were going with him.

The students were in their places when the lecturer came into the room. Many of them knew of the tragedy which had struck their chief during the holidays so there was unusual silence as he came in with his lecture notes, and arranged them on the lectern. Minoru noticed the drawn look and the unnatural pallor of his face. The old bounce was lacking but the learned doctor, sticking more closely to his notes than usual, managed to get on with the lecture as if nothing had crushed his world.

After it was over, and the men were rushing to their next assignments, Minoru stood to one side keeping his eyes on his father's face, waiting to see if there would be a chance for a word with him in private. David stood gathering his notes together when Minoru came to stand beside him.

"Dr. McLean, it is good to have you back with us to guide our studies. We have missed you. I, too, sorrow for Betsy."

David McLean lifted his tired, sad eyes to find the tall Japanese man standing before him with the light of love in his face. David McLean could not at that moment have described what it was that he sensed about this extraordinary fellow.

"Thank you, Dr. Tada, and thank you for being with us when we needed you that awful morning. By the way, if you have a minute, will you please step into my office? I want to look up the schedules for operations. Yours is first in line, so it should be coming up soon."

Once in the office, David McLean consulted his schedule, raised his head to look into Minoru's handsome face, "You and I are to make a team on March 9 at nine thirty in the morning. Heart operation, as I've told you. The patient has been building up strength for some weeks now and before that date, you will become acquainted with her, she with you. You and I will go over this thing step by step. It is nothing to dread, especially for you. You did almost this same operation in Japan simply by following steps outlined in the American Medical Journal."

"With you, Dr. McLean, I fear no operation. I will look forward to our date." He shook hands with the doctor and had a wild desire to skip from the room like a child. He could not get to his room fast enough to check the date on his calendar. The idea of having a chance to assist his illustrious father in an operation was more than he could take with true Japanese control.

The days passed more quickly than Minoru had thought possible. Several times he had gone to visit with the frail woman who looked at him with mingled admiration and questioning in her eyes. He could almost see her mind at work. *It will probably really not matter who assists in this operation. Dr. McLean will do the job, and if there is a chance, humanly speaking, then he will give me mine.*

Minoru woke earlier than usual on the morning of the scheduled operation. He lay quietly going over the steps as Dr. McLean had instructed him. The pinched face of the patient swam before him as he thought of the responsibility of a surgeon who takes such a frail life into his hands. He began to pray for the little mother who so desperately wanted to return to her family; he prayed for each of the four doctors who would be there for the operation, and for the nurses who would assist. He asked, as always, that Divine power would flow through Dr. McLean and the assistants and that a strength, which could not be humanly generated, be given them.

He wondered about what Dr. McLean's thoughts were on such a morning. If one did not have Divine strength to draw from at such a time, where did one turn? Was it possible for a surgeon to have unlimited confidence in his own powers? Minoru lay a long time thinking about these things.

When Minoru walked into the surgery behind Dr. McLean, all was in readiness for the operation; the student observers were in their places, the anesthetist was at his post, the other two doctors were there. The patient, with chest exposed, lay as one who had just died. Minoru felt that he was entering an arena where was to be fought a battle of Life against Death.

He gave the chief of surgeons a swift glance, and noticed that the eyes above the mask were troubled, his brow was deathly pale. Minoru looked down just as the surgeon opened his hand for the first instrument and detected a perceptible tremor where there should have been complete control.

With clocklike precision Minoru concentrated upon his duties and studiedly refrained from looking at his teacher-surgeon. After the incision was made and the by-pass in the aorta had been secured; that split second before the critical thrust with the scalpel was to be made Minoru felt, rather than heard, his father give a deep, desperate sigh. It was almost a sob. He pressed close to hear the words muffled by the mask, "Dr. Tada, you will have to take over. I am not well." So saying he moved aside for Minoru. He felt himself stepping into the place vacated by his father as the resident surgeon moved into the assistant's position.

There was slight flurry of panic in the room. For a second, Minoru felt as if he were going to faint. Miraculously his head cleared and he proceeded with his work without another qualm.

Somewhere, in the midst of the operation, when the worst was over and the patient was responding splendidly, Minoru glanced around to find that his father had gone from the room. The resident surgeon was helping him with expert precision. There was nothing to worry about; the patient had come through the ordeal and the critical stage of the process was passed. There was a good chance that the little woman would make the grade.

Minoru's eyes flooded with tears of thankfulness as he turned into the anteroom from the surgery. He removed his gloves, mask and robe and wiped both sweat and tears from his face.

When he saw the patient rolled into the recovery room, Minoru went in search of Dr. McLean. The girl in his office reported that he had been admitted to the hospital as a patient. He located the room and peeked in to find Dr. McLean sleeping under sedation.

"Heart?" he asked the nurse in charge.

"Nervous exhaustion, I think. Dr. Hughes does not seem worried about him."

"I'll be back to see him in the late afternoon," Minoru said.

When he came back in the afternoon, he found David McLean lying with his eyes open but his thoughts seemed far away. When he saw Minoru he held out his hand to him.

"How did it go after I flubbed the job, Dr. Tada?"

"The patient fared better than I did, at first. Doctor, when you stepped back to leave me, I almost fainted for the first time in my life. If I had known that you had left the room, I am sure I should have fallen on the floor without passing the knife to Dr. Hughes."

Minoru gave a sharp laugh of pure relief. "The patient fared better than either of us. She seems to be coming around splendidly. We've nothing to worry about now. How about you? How do you feel?"

"I hardly know. I expect to be taken home tomorrow. Want to be in my own bed for I'm definitely not a hospital patient so have no right to clutter a bed. I'm not myself — that is all I know at the moment.

"Thank you for taking over for me and doing such a splendid job. That was a shocking way to treat a student, but I had no control over anything at that moment." He turned his head away and looked at the wall.

Minoru patted his shoulder affectionately and walked from the room. Rest was now the best medicine for his exhausted father, Dr. Tada decided.

22

SOMETIME DURING the morning of the next day at the Medical Center, a note was slipped into Minoru's hand. When he opened it he was surprised to see that it was from Dr. McLean.

Dr. Tada:
Could you manage to drop by my hospital room in early afternoon? I want to see you for just a minute.

Thank you,

Minoru did not have the time to wonder about it. He had checked their patient twice during the morning, and all was progressing satisfactorily and he had asked that Dr. McLean be given the reports also. He stuffed the note in his pocket and registered the request in his memory.

When he tip-toed into the hospital room after his lunch, he found Dr. McLean dressed, ready to return home.

"I know you think it strange that I asked to see you, but, after your visit yesterday afternoon, I hatched an idea that I want to present to you."

Minoru's eyes grew round with anticipation. "It just occurred to me that when I get home, except for Mrs. Hayes, my housekeeper, and the man who works about the grounds during the daytime, I shall be alone. At night, I shall be completely alone — and — somehow, I don't seem to be able to face that prospect. Would you consider leaving your convenient place at my sister's and coming to be with me for a time?"

This was wholly unexpected by Minoru; something that he could not have dreamed up. His mind raced like a tape recorder going in reverse, but, before he could find words for an answer, Dr. McLean continued, "I know that you do not have a car. Do you drive?"

"No, and I was just thinking that I would have no way to get back and forth to the Center. I have never owned a car, so I do not drive."

"That won't matter. My man can be your chauffeur — take you in the mornings and come for you in the afternoons. It will be a great favor to me if you feel that you could keep me company at nights for a few weeks."

Minoru was too overcome with emotion to answer at once. His face was flushed with pleasure; his tongue would not function. Finally he managed.

"It would be a great pleasure for me, Dr. McLean. If I can help you I'll be happy. When would you want me to come?"

"I'd like you to go home with me at three this afternoon, if possible. If you can pack your things before then, we will take them along; if not, then Jake can come back for them later. Are you free to go this afternoon?"

"Yes, as it happens. I will go now to pack. Shall I wait at Miss Julia's?"

"Yes, that is wonderful — wonderful of you to be so kind. Wait at Julia's and we'll pick you up sometime around three. It will be great to be home tonight."

When Minoru left the hospital, there was a queer feeling in the pit of his stomach. Questions began to swarm his mind: why did he ask me? Why not Dr. Bond or Dr. Hughes who have been his friends for years?

Minoru knew now the feeling of a dog made happy by his master and cannot seem to wag his tail fast enough to express his pleasure. This mental picture of himself made him laugh aloud as he bounded across the campus to Miss Julia's.

He was ready when the long black car came to a stop before the gate. Dr. McLean still had the drawn look about his eyes, and there was a slight tremor as he held out his hand to welcome Minoru into the car beside him.

This is not good, but a complete rest will bring him out of it. The passing of time will soften the blow which caved in his world, Minoru thought as they rode along.

Conversing very little on the trip, they were content to watch Jake steer the car expertly around the curves of the hill until the long, silent house burst upon their sight. Mrs. Hayes was there to open the door to them and to express her solicitude.

"I have your room all ready, Doctor," she said. She turned to Minoru, "Young man, will you see him up to his room while I get some hot coffee? That will help to pick him up; it usually does."

Before Minoru could offer his support for climbing the stairs, David McLean put his arm through Minoru's strong one and together they slowly began the climb. In the spacious bedroom, David McLean sank thankfully into a deep armchair by the window and looked about the room registering happiness over being at home.

"Minoru, you are to have the room next to mine. It was my wife's room, but things have been shifted about in there since she was here. It will put you in calling distance during the night."

Jake came in with Minoru's bag and stood in the middle of the floor waiting instructions.

"Take the bag through that door, Jake, into the next room. Dr. Tada will be sleeping there." The doctor smiled a weak smile into Minoru's eyes, "I hope I won't disturb your rest during the nights, but it will be comforting to know that you are there in case I need professional help rather than companionship."

The doctor seemed so tired, Minoru insisted that he allow them to get him settled in bed. When he was comfortably settled, Mrs. Hayes came in with his coffee. Jake brought the accumulated mail of the past two days and put it on the table beside his bed.

Minoru went into his room and began to sense the strangeness of the place as well as the situation. This was going to be an experience worth describing in his letter to Matsuko. Something about this was weaving a feeling of unreality about him.

With Jake's prompt cooperation, Minoru carried on his work at the Center by day and acted as a companion for his father at night. David McLean seemed too content to lie in bed. When Minoru came in the late afternoon, he insisted that the Doctor be dressed for a short walk around the grounds. Because he knew this was wise, David was habitually dressed though he found that he was interested in very little that went on about him. He was gray in the face with his neck wasting away. At first his medical friends came often, but, as the weeks passed, they began to wonder among themselves if David McLean would ever pull back and be able to return to his place among them.

Minoru, too, was concerned. He did not feel that he could consult the medical men about his father. Once he did ask Dr. Bond's opinion, and realized that he received a frank answer, "David McLean will never get any better unless he tries to help himself. Life caves in on a lot of people; they get up and try again. David seems content to let the collapsed sky cover him completely. His daughter's death was shockingly tragic, but, if he would look about him, he would discover that this has happened to a great many people, as any surgeon knows. Many of us have passed through these valleys of shadows. I am really as surprised as anyone over David's reaction."

"What is he like at home, Dr. Tada? You are more closely associated with him than we are — you are with him every evening. How does he seem to you?"

"He seems to me," Minoru said solemnly, "he seems as if something has died inside of him."

Dr. Bond gave this young doctor a shrewd look, and turned away feeling that his description of David McLean was an apt one — and tragic.

David began to encourage Dr. McLean's staying up for dinner. Mrs. Hayes always did her best to tempt his appetite. She did her part in the only way that she knew. Always she set the dining room table, a bit more festive than usual. Minoru began insisting that they go into the den after dinner rather than back to the bedroom. For, once in his room, Dr. McLean sought the soft comfort of his bed.

Beside the den fire, David McLean spoke slowly to his young companion.

"Minoru, I am not getting better here at home. In some ways I'm discouraged. I have been thinking about going down to Florida for some sun and fishing. I am a good fisherman, or used to be. Maybe out on the bay at St. Petersburg I might take a new lease on life. What do you think about it?"

Being a Japanese made it hard for Minoru to be frank. Yet, as he sat looking at the doctor, he knew that honesty was called for.

"Will you excuse me for being honest in my answer? Do you truly want my opinion?"

David McLean had never seen the composed Japanese in this mood before. "I do want to know what you think, Minoru. You don't think I am getting better here do you?"

"I know that you do not grow better."

"Well, what about the trip? Do you think it's a good idea? You know about Florida, don't you? You know that it is warm there all winter."

"Yes, I know about Florida, but I am wondering if it is only sunshine that you need. Florida will not cure *your* illness; it might help.

"The sun warms the body but it takes the love of God's Son to warm the heart. That I think you need most of all. He gives us Life."

If Minoru had thrown a bucket of ice water in his father's face, David could not have been more astonished. Never had anyone talked to him like this before. Who would have thought that an Oriental, with a Buddhist background, would be the first to speak to him of God's Son in this personal relationship? That he would be the first to put his finger on the sore spot of his spirit.

"You are a Christian, Minoru?" he asked.

"Yes. Once God spoke to me very clearly. Would you like for me to tell you?" Somehow David McLean wanted to hear this more than anything. Minoru began to recount his experience simply. As he talked he noticed that Dr. McLean's chin was trembling, and, fearing that this might be too emotional for a sick man, Minoru hurriedly sketched the experience in the dissecting laboratory. He ended by asking the question, "Dr. McLean, you do not have this strength in your life, do you?"

"No, Minoru, not in the way that you have spoken of it. What an amazing experience.

"I grew up surrounded by Christ's teachings but they never penetrated my life. In my present state of sheer weakness, do you think this Light, this strength, of which you speak, would do any-thing for me?"

"It can make you whole again. It can make you the great surgeon you once were, and completely restore you to full physical strength with an added spiritual vitality which is not now yours."

There followed a period of questioning and answering such as neither had experienced before: the great surgeon questioning; the young doctor speaking from things already experienced in his own life.

"We are two men of science, Doctor. When we are training to be doctors, we were told to make experiments for ourselves. Is it too much then, to ask you to do that now in the test tube of your life? Are you willing to try this before taking off to the sunshine of St. Petersburg?"

David McLean had to admit the good sense of this suggestion. Before the month of March was over, their daily periods of studying the Bible together, the discussions concerning the doubts, fears, stumbling blocks which seemed to hurl themselves across Dr. McLean's frail and halting faith, brought little progress. David McLean began to feel a new awareness though there seemed to be a clogging somewhere which brooked no by-passing.

When he spoke of this to Minoru one night, the young doctor smiled and said, "This open channel to God is not like the diseased aorta of the heart. It cannot be unclogged by a by-pass and an operation. That blockage — that clogging, as you call it — is unacknowledged sin in your life. This is what Christ came to free us from; He alone can make clean this channel to God."

"Did you have something of the same experience, Minoru?"

"Of course. The very first thing that God revealed to me was the fact that my spiritual *aorta* was clogged with hate." Having said this, Minoru blushed like a schoolboy caught with a frog in his pocket. David saw this and laughed.

"You, hating, Minoru? That is hard for me to believe; you are the most peaceful of persons in your inner man."

"I had my reason for hating then; the reason still exists but the miracle of God's love has shown me a better way. In hating I was simply destroying myself." Minoru was near tears when he said these words, as he sat looking at the object of his once bitter hatred. He marveled at his own ability to have said these things without giving the whole story away.

There followed more talk, more explanations, more trying to be reasonable. Minoru said as he turned to leave the room for the night, "I want you to read the third chapter of John's gospel tonight. Put yourself in Nicodemus' place, as you read, and let Jesus reason with you. You will then see that new birth does not come to one by reasoning; it is a thing of the Spirit. One must throw himself upon the never-failing mercy of God. The Holy Spirit will do the rest."

David McLean nodded his agreement and thanked him for the evening.

"You're a good diagnostician as well as a good surgeon, Minoru. At least I feel that you have understood my case. I'll take the medicine prescribed. What was it again?"

Minoru reached for the Bible and opened it at the third chapter of John's gospel.

"Here," he said handing the doctor the book, "take this in one dose and we'll see how it works for you." He smiled at his father, who at this moment, was not an eminent surgeon of the great medical center. He was a pajama-clad man in deep need, lying on his bed without the strength to rise and meet life's demands.

23

THE NEXT DAY, when Minoru stopped at Miss Julia's to pick up his mail, he found, as he had hoped and expected, a letter from Matsuko. He sat down to read it.

> My Dearest Minoru:
>
> I have an overpowering desire to see you. I feel a great need of some time with you before our wedding and we set off together to the other side of the world. I am not uncertain on any score where you are concerned, my darling. I do not doubt my love in any way — it's, well maybe it is because I love you so much that I feel this great need to be with you. Such a revolutionary step in my life needs the reassurance which only you can give to me, not through letters but in person. I have been trying to work out some plan whereby we may be together for a few days.
>
> I have one week of vacation in April. Do you suppose that you could somehow squeeze in a long weekend and fly out here? Have you any suggestions from your end of the line? I know how tightly things will be wound for you during these last few busy weeks, but there should be someway for us to see each other.

Minoru had been wishing for this very thing. Most of their wedding plans had been made by letter, an unsatisfactory method when so much was involved. Besides wanting to see Matsuko again, there were certain plans which needed to be discussed face to face; there was the date of sailing and his idea that they would take a long trip through Europe rather than the direct route across the Pacific Ocean. Yet, how could a medical fellow, in the last push before the end, find time? *This,* Minoru thought, *has been the cry of all medical men since the beginning.*

This problem kept popping up in his mind all day as he searched for loopholes to allow a visit with Matsuko. He was rereading her letter while Jake drove him up the hill to the McLean home; he almost jumped when Jake exclaimed, "Look at those woods. There's a rash of dogwood ready to whiten them up, some of these mornings."

Minoru looked where Jake was pointing and saw the burgeoning signs of Spring all about him. Spring was definitely being warmed back and the grip of Winter was being loosened on the world.

As they turned into the driveway, Minoru wondered if his father had begun to feel some of the thaw in the frozen core of his being. He mounted the stairs two at a time in his impatience to see how things had gone with him during the day. He found his patient dressed and ready for a walk in the woods. There was a new spring in his step as they followed the bridle path about the estate.

When they were deep in the woods Minoru could feel Nature's

urge to free herself from the winter's bondage. He studied David McLean's face to see if he too were feeling the wonder of it. He was. It was reflected in his face.

"Minoru, I feel a kinship with these woods today," the doctor suddenly confided, "While I was reading and rereading the prescribed chapter in John's gospel today, there seemed to be a sort of swelling within me, just as I see in the trees about us. Does that sound silly to you?"

"Not at all. Go ahead, tell me."

"I did as you said, I became Nicodemus in my imagination and I asked a few questions on my own — some that Nicodemus never thought about. The answers which came to me were astounding. I am not sure I can tell you about them."

"Maybe they're not meant to be told to anyone. Don't try, just keep them to yourself. Keep up the spiritual exercises and one day you will step out into the open before your Maker. That will be *your* day!"

They walked on in silence, communicating without words. Minoru felt that this was the first step toward health. He noticed a spot of color in the doctor's pale cheek and his heart gave a great surge of thankfulness.

After dinner that night, Minoru read part of Matsuko's letter to David McLean. Before he read it, he spoke of his concern in the matter she presented to him. Dr. McLean knew of the wedding plans and had been interested in all that Minoru had seen fit to share with him about their romance. He felt flattered that Minoru was bringing him a problem; immediately he began to wrestle with it.

"You are just beginning to feel the strait-jacket which medicine has thrust upon you, Minoru. Life hardly gives a doctor a chance to choose his own mate. There is no use for you to ask for time for the trip at the Center. They feel that now you're about to leave, they have a claim on your body and soul. But, the fact stands, you do need to see your girl, and she needs to be with you." He sat in silence weighing things.

"Minoru, why can't Matsuko fly here and stay with us for a week? Mrs. Hayes could move in with us too. We could have a good time together. It would give Matsuko a chance to see this part of the country, and you two could have every evening together. How about that?"

This was a brand new solution to Minoru; he was intrigued with the idea. This was not exactly the way a Japanese would have handled things, but it made excellent good sense to him.

"You are sure that this would be all right with you? That having her would not upset you in any way?" Minoru was showing his gratitude by the deep pools of lights in his eyes.

"Sure, I'm sure. I'd like to know the girl who's to be your wife. This will be my chance. I could show her the city by day; you would be with her in the evenings." His smile was so relaxed and sincere, Minoru was pleased on two counts.

"Write your girl tonight extending the invitation. Maybe you'd best keep the plan of where she is to stay a secret. Let that be a surprise for her."

Before Minoru left his father's room that night, David McLean abruptly asked him, "Was Matsuko the reason you stopped seeing Betsy? Were you in love with Matsuko at that time?"

Minoru was too taken by surprise to answer at once. "Betsy and I were never anything but friends, Doctor, but, at that time I had not met Matsuko. I met her on our trip last summer. I never knew that you were ever aware of the fact that Betsy and I knew each other."

"Yes, I knew. Julia told me first, then Betsy spoke of it after you stopped seeing each other. When I first heard of it, I was shocked by the idea that if it were serious, you might be carting Betsy off to Japan. Of course, it will be the same for Matsuko for she is American, too, but with a difference since she is also Japanese. I want you to know, Minoru, that I never opposed Betsy's seeing you. Why did you stop?"

"There were many things, Doctor. For one thing I have never believed in mixed marriages. It is too hard on the children. Someday, before I leave for home, I will tell you how near I came to being wrecked by the fact of my birth. Betsy and I were too different in every way. We were just friends. I felt more like a brother than . . ." here Minoru cut his words short, as if he had said too much already.

"I failed with Betsy. I failed miserably. During this time of enforced rest, I have had much time to think — too much time," David McLean said.

"How do you think you failed Betsy?"

"Something impresses itself upon me — and I have a great sense of failure in my personal life — as a father — so many ways." He ran his hand over his face as if trying to rub away the unpleasant things which clogged his mind.

"God forgives failures as well as sins. That's part of the great gift of salvation."

They spoke no more about this but turned their talk to other things before separating for the night.

Minoru went to bed happier than he had been in a long time: Matsuko would come soon; Dr. McLean was having time to look into the hidden recesses of his memory and was being shown his needs. Minoru felt that it was only a matter of time before his father would come into the full beam of God's light and love and be able to rise again, a man full of power.

As Jake drove Minoru to meet Matsuko's plane, the world was awash with Spring's glory. Minoru had never felt so alive, so purposeful or so brimming with happiness. He knew that his life would be complete when Matsuko became his bride. Looking up at the blue, blue sky above he whispered silently, "How very wonderful You are, God! How wonderfully good!"

He felt that his heart would explode with sheer joy at the sight of her stepping from the plane. When she reached him, his true Japanese reserve forced him to keep his greeting formal. He bowed to Matsuko from his waist, but she knew, from watching her parents over the years, how deep were his feelings of love for her. *So long as a woman knows,* she thought to herself as she ran her arm through his to feel his nearness, *she has the deepest secret of life.*

Minoru had never mentioned in his letters the fact that he was being driven by a chauffeur. When Jake came to get her bags to take them to the car, she lifted an eyebrow and whispered, "How now, Duke?" Minoru blushed, smiled but said nothing.

As they drove along, he began to tell her of the plans made for her stay. She knew from his letters why he was staying with the illustrious surgeon. He now tried to prepare her for the experience. "At first, when I moved to the McLean home, everything about it seemed strange and incongruous to me, but after these weeks of staying there, I am beginning to feel at home — actually at home."

As he was saying this, he pointed to the house on the hill now gradually being hidden from sight by the new leaves of the trees in Spring dress.

"Feel at home in that house!" Matsuko exclaimed, "Hardly, Dr. Tada."

When Mrs. Hayes let them into the foyer, Matsuko looked about with the same sort of awe Minoru remembered feeling the morning he and Miss Julia had come to wait for the doctor's arrival from the hospital. She looked up to see understanding amusement shining in Minoru's face.

Mrs. Hayes showed her up to her room and left to return to her duties below. Matsuko wandered about knowing that it had once been Betsy's room. She also wondered how it would be to live in such a place permanently.

At the dinner table that evening, Matsuko looked up suddenly at the two men who sat about the table with her, and had a strange feeling that there was a striking resemblance between the two of them. She did not voice it, for the men were in a discussion which could not be interrupted. Her eyes left their faces and dropped to their hands. Here the similarity was even more striking. For a moment she put down her fork and stared at the two in silence. She shook her head as if denying the thought which had crept there unawares! *It couldn't be, It couldn't be. I'm sure Minoru would have told me,* she kept repeating to herself.

Minoru got off to the Center before Matsuko was awake the next morning. The last push before the holidays at the Nursing School had been tiring, and the trip had been her first on a plane, so she slept until mid-morning.

It became the part of each day's ritual for Dr. McLean to get down to have breakfast with the house guest. Afterwards, they took a long drive through the city; Jake drove while the doctor pointed out the various places of interest.

After the dinner hour, the evenings were spent in the den. The doctor left them there, knowing that was the room in which they felt most at home.

Neither of the young people had ever known such happiness as was theirs during those evenings in the room where they could feel at home with each other.

On Matsuko's last day, while she was breakfasting with the doctor, they had just been discussing Minoru's promising future as a surgeon, when David McLean said suddenly, "I'm frank to say, Matsuko, he is just as fine a man as he is a surgeon, and that's saying a great deal. I could wish that Minoru were my son. In fact, if he would agree to staying here, I would adopt him. I'd adopt you, too, of course," he quickly added, laughing.

"The other night, at the table, while you two were talking, Dr. McLean, I had a sudden feeling that there was something very similar between the two of you. Really, I'm not joking. There is the same shape to your faces, the same wave in your hair, the same bone structure — and your hands! Have you ever looked at Minoru's hands? They are perfect replicas of your own. Maybe surgeons grow to be alike as husbands and wives are supposed to do."

David McLean had not laughed so heartily in months as over this. He knew that having this sparkling young woman about was good for him.

That night at the dinner table, David McLean repeated the things which Matsuko had told him at breakfast. Minoru laughed over them, too, but there was a flush about his face which David McLean took to be a flush of pleasure in the compliment.

"Matsuko says surgeons grow to look alike. Isn't that an idea? I wish she could see Bond and me together." The idea of his looking like the square-cut Dr. Bond made both men laugh more heartily.

The topic of conversation was switched by Minoru to the happenings at the Medical Center. Matsuko and David soon forgot the talk of similarities, but Minoru kept the thought active in his mind. Could this be the opportune time that he had been waiting for to break the secret wide open? No, he must first make sure that the doctor was well enough to absorb the shock of it. Nothing must happen to send his noticeable progress spinning to a fall.

David McLean, realizing that this was the last night the couple would have together, excused himself and went to his room.

Minoru had kept well his secret of the long trek about Europe which was to give them a honeymoon to remember all of their lives. When they were alone in the den, he drew out the brochure of the trip and handed it to Matsuko. As she looked at it, he said, "That is our itinerary, darling. We are going home the long way around — New York, England, Scotland, France, Germany with a little bit of Rome — then around by the ports. We'll be old married people by the time we reach Takarazuka."

Matsuko could not believe that he was telling the truth. Such a thing had never occurred to her. She had thought it wonderful that he could afford to take her across the Pacific Ocean.

"Minoru — are you sure we can afford this? It's wonderful! If it *is* true, instead of going home to get the wedding plans in line, I'll leave that to Mother, while I get myself informed enough for all of this. It will take weeks! Minoru, I could never have dreamed anything so wonderful. Are you sure that I'm not dreaming?" she asked from the circle of his embrace.

"I'm not quite sure, Matsuko, that everything is not a dream. This has been a week beyond all dreaming. Please make me feel that your being here is real and that this happiness will be ours as long as we live."

Matsuko did her very best to convince him.

24

THE MORNING AFTER Matsuko left for home, the big house on the hill seemed strangely empty and silent. After breakfasting alone, David McLean climbed the stairs to his bedroom feeling that life had suddenly fled from the house. Mrs. Hayes went quietly about her own duties downstairs, getting things back to normal after their guest had departed.

Sitting by his window, which gave him a broad sweep of the grounds now in spring dress, David McLean mused on all that had taken place since the arrival of Matsuko Hara. There had been much about this lovely Japanese girl which reminded him of Michiko Takahashi; the same jet-black hair, the same bruised-magnolia blossom skin, and tip-tilted eyes which gave to her the look of a pixie. Before he could corral his roving thoughts, he was back in memory living again those days of 1939. In former times, when those vagrant thoughts had cropped up in his mind, he had been able to rationalize the thing he had done to the wonderful Japanese girl who had loved him, and whom he had left with a promise never fulfilled. Now he could not justify his actions, for when he had told her good-by, he had every intention of returning to take her to America as his bride. "Why didn't I?" he asked aloud.

Then he remembered that after his first day at sea, he became acquainted with a group of American young people on board the ship. Their activities were in full swing; he had joined them in the evenings. This was the familiar world to him — a world that could never belong to Michiko. Before he had reached Honolulu, he knew that his parents had been right in opposing his marriage, and that he would never return to Japan.

"Why didn't I write to tell her so?" That question stung him. Before this, he had always been able to push these thoughts back into the dark recesses of his mind as something which need not be faced. Somehow, until this morning, Michiko's side of the affair had not been fully examined. Now there was no getting away from the thing. *The girl truly loved me! How deeply she must have been hurt by the curtain of silence which I deliberately let fall! What an awful thing I did to her! What a heel I am and was!* He found himself mopping beads of perspiration from his brow, while memories kept coming.

Once he was home again, the world had seemed so different, yet so familiar and right to him; mentally and emotionally he had clipped every string which might have drawn him back to Japan and Michiko. He never mentioned his love affair to his parents after his return; they never brought up the subject either.

At once Julia had busied herself to see that he was drawn back into the social whirl of Cleveland. When he met Julia's best friend, Martha Moss, she seemed the girl who would best fit into his life as a budding surgeon; so there was a hurried courtship, and Martha became his bride.

He tried to cut short this torture, and get on with the spiritual exercises outlined by Dr. Tada. What was the expression he had used? "Keep on letting the wind of the Spirit play over you, one day you will step out into God's light."

It was not working this morning. Everywhere he turned he could see Michiko's face. The rebuke was more than he could take. It was as if the memories so long pushed back, suddenly had been dredged from the hidden places of his soul-like evil bubbles of gas rising from a stagnant pond. These things which he had rationalized away through the years, rose now as loathsome evils.

He saw them in their true light this morning, and was stifled by them. He found himself going, almost without knowing where, out into the soft spring air. Once out of the house, he felt that a good brisk walk would be good for him. He headed into the woods rioting with spring, and was gone a long time.

In the late afternoon, David McLean was watching from his window when Jake stopped the car at the front door, and Minoru literally sprang out and bounded up the front steps.

Soon he will have to move back to Julia's for those last days at the Center. How I dread for the time to come! David McLean moaned to himself.

Minoru came into the room to find how the day had gone for him, then hurried into his own room to get ready for dinner. Mrs. Hayes liked promptness; he always tried to adhere to her schedule.

I wonder if anyone who is in love, who is young and bursting with life, knows how truly blessed he is? David McLean mused. Seeing Minoru Tada bound into his room for a minute, made him believe that here was one young man who knew.

During the dinner hour, Minoru told of seeing Matsuko off on the plane. He tried to express his thanks to David for making possible the wonderful week together, and to tell him what being together had meant to them.

"It meant a great deal to me too, Minoru. That girl of yours is a jewel. You're a fortunate pair; I congratulate you. Now, tell me something of your wedding plans."

"According to Matsuko, the wedding will be very simple — a small church affair. Her parents are true Japanese so all will be very simple but in excellent taste. Matsuko is having only one attendant; I'm to have a best man. I might as well ask you now, will you stand beside me on July twenty-fifth as my best man?"

"Now look here, Minoru," David began to protest, "I think one's best man should be a young friend, not an old man, old enough to be the groom's father."

"Often," Minoru defended his choice, "young men have their own fathers. Age has nothing to do with it and you *are* my best friend."

David McLean, the great surgeon, the eminent doctor, blushed with pride at this remark.

"Put like that, Dr. Tada, how could I possibly turn you down?

Count on me to be beside you; and your wedding date will help me decide the day that I shall plan to return to the Medical Center. I shall go back on August first."

Minoru's heart gave a bound. "Then you think that you are ready to face that again, to get back into harness? Wonderful, wonderful, Doctor!"

"I know now," David McLean said solemnly, "that I can go back with new strength flowing through me. With that, I cannot fail. I think I stepped into His beam of light today, Minoru. I feel now that I shall never again have to walk in darkness."

"Tell me about it."

They continued to sit at the table after Mrs. Hayes had cleared it, and they heard the kitchen door latch after her as she left for the night. It seemed easier to talk facing each other across the table, so they continued to sit.

"Was there a sudden stepping out into the open, or was it a gradual thing?" Minoru asked him.

"Gradual over these past weeks, I think, though just this morning from the depth of my being, there rose a bubble of sin which broke wide open before me. I was shocked at the enormity of the thing. Let me begin at the beginning, Minoru:

"Did you ever wonder why you were chosen for the fellowship here at the Center? There were dozens of applications from all over the world."

Minoru sat with his heart in his throat, wondering if all the while David McLean had known about his son. He sat listening in silence.

"It was I, one of the committee to choose the fellows, who insisted that one of the three fellowships be given to you. It was because you were from the little town of Takarazuka, a little town that I had known and loved back in 1939."

At this point, Minoru deliberately rose from his chair and went to turn off the brilliant overhead lights and to turn on a small lamp beside the buffet which cast a subdued light over the room. Minoru wanted no expression which might flit across his face to interrupt the telling of this story.

David McLean thought nothing of this change of the lighting but kept right on with the story.

"I told Matsuko, and perhaps I've told you, that I spent a short while in Japan in 1939. I really was there to study in Kyoto for a while, but I spent a great deal of time in Takarazuka — your city. At the great theater there I met an exquisite little Japanese girl. I fell deeply in love with her; she with me. She belonged to a good family and was their only child. She spoke some English, enough to let me understand that our love would never be understood by her family, so I never met them.

"I also knew that my parents would not approve, though I wrote them that I intended bringing Michiko home with me as my bride. They hit the ceiling! My dad wrote a letter calculated to reel me in. He succeeded, for I at once decided that it would be better to go home without a bride, settle with the family, then return for her."

Here David McLean paused in the telling of the story, ran his hand over his face as if trying to wipe off the dreadful memories. He rose and paced about the room, pausing now and again to take a deep breath to still the passions which made him weak. Minoru sat still, unmoving, with his hand shading his eyes.

David McLean was able, little by little, to get the whole story told: their secret meetings, Michiko's acceptance of the reason for his return home, the promise to come again and take her with him to America, and, after many stops and starts, the mention of their last night together when Michiko had given him all that a woman in love can give. He told of the fading of the affair, like a dream at the day's beginning.

"Before I reached home, there seemed to be absolutely no substance to this Japanese interlude. I simply let the whole thing vanish and silence fall between me and the girl whom I loved and who truly loved me."

It was a long and painful recital. "You know, Minoru, until I began letting the Holy Spirit have His way with me, as you instructed, I had never seen this thing for what it actually is and was. This morning after Matsuko left, the whole thing rose up to smite me. It literally drove me out into the woods because I was trying to run away from it. I was too proud to stay in my room and humble myself before God for an all-out confession which I knew was the thing I'd be forced to do.

"Once in the woods, I suddenly saw God in everything! The beauty of the woods, familiar to me for over twenty years, became too much for me. I did not return to the house for fear of having the mood escape me. I fell upon my knees beside the big rocks at the back of the lot, and made a clean sweep of everything. I tell you, my boy, I have never experienced such inner peace, such assurance of God's forgiving power, love and understanding. This is what you have been hoping and praying for all the time, isn't it?"

He turned abruptly to face Minoru and found the young man's face bathed in tears. Without a word, Minoru rose from the table and left the room. David McLean was stunned. He did not know what to think. His mind was whirling at a rapid rate as he continued to pace the floor.

When Minoru came back into the room he carried the canvas packet which Obasan had handed him after his grandfather's funeral.

"I have something here I want to read to you, Dr. McLean, then you will understand why I am so emotionally involved in this story you have told me." He drew out his grandfather's letter and began to translate it into English. Several times during the reading, the doctor put his head upon his arms folded upon the table, to weep long, racking sobs. As the truth began to unfold in the old man's heartbroken words, he looked up at the young man across the table from him. He did not interrupt the reading but stared at Minoru in unbelief.

When the letter was finished, Minoru folded it and put it back in the packet. "Now you *know*," he said simply, "I am really your son."

David McLean sat for a moment in stunned silence, then, reached impulsively across the table to take Minoru's hand into his own.

"Can it be? Can it be? My son! Minoru, you are actually my son? It was so obvious that even Matsuko recognized the resemblance and yet I have been blind."

"I had not told her anything, so she must have seen it. While you were influencing the committee to choose the young man from Takarazuka, he was in Takarazuka scheming to get to the city where his father was chief of surgeons. All of my life I have dreamed of meeting with the man who wronged my mother — all of my boyhood was spent in planning ways to get even with the despised person who deserved all the evil things my boyish mind could devise. You and I have God to thank for His intervention. When He touched my life in the dissecting room, all the hate was drained from me, and His Love took over. I have known about you for ten years. All the plans to come to you have been worth my while since, by your own admission, you truly loved my mother. It makes quite a difference to me that I was conceived in love. How wonderful to have heard the story from you!"

While Dr. McLean sat in silence, holding his head in his hands, Minoru sketched his childhood overshadowed by a grandfather whose heart had been broken. It was such an evening as neither of the two were ever to forget.

Hours ticked away while they sat together letting questions and answers fly back and forth between them. There were many things that David had to know. Many things which Minoru was determined that he *should* know. David McLean sat holding the old kodak picture of himself and the slender Japanese girl, and read aloud the words in his own writing on the back of it, "David M. McLean, M.D., Cleveland, Ohio."

"That," Minoru told him "was the slender thread I used to trace you and the fact that I knew that you were a doctor."

"Did that have anything to do with your desire to study medicine? From what your grandfather said in the letter, you always wanted to become a doctor."

"I suppose you must have left that much of an impact upon me, for I wanted to be a doctor long before I knew anything about you. You have said yourself, when there was no cause for you to be prejudiced, that I *am* a good doctor," Minoru turned to his father with an impish grin.

"You are just that — and one to be proud of, my son. Now, where do we go from here, Minoru? I feel like a prodigal father returning to a worthy son. What can I do to make up, in part, for all the anguish I have caused you? How can I claim you, now that I have found you?" He sounded so desperate as he paced back and forth in the room, that Minoru tried to calm him.

"I have been thinking over things, Doctor, for I knew the time would come for this revealing of myself to you. I have thought it all through. If this were made public now it could do great damage to you — much hurt. There is no need for that. I am now a man. Let's leave it a secret to the world. I shall return to Japan in a few months, you will again take your place as chief of surgeons, respected and admired. Our relationship as father and son was established in love actually, far better than most sons and fathers are able to establish it in a lifetime together. Let's let it stand at that."

David could not speak at once. "What about your name? I'd like for you to go back to Japan declaring to the world that you are legally my son."

"I've thought about that too. I shall return to Japan as David Minoru Tada — the name my mother gave me when I was born. The David will be for you, and, for me to know it is enough. Tada is a name to which I am giving content. After all, I am known in my hometown by that name. I think I'd prefer to keep it for I *am* Japanese."

"Do you feel that you must go back to Japan, Minoru? Why not stay here and work with me? I don't care what people say or think. It would mean everything for me to have you near."

"I am a Japanese, Doctor. I could never be anything else. I feel that my country needs what I now have to give. Planes fly across the Pacific. You can come over to see us. We can never be but a matter of hours apart. One day we shall walk the streets of Takarazuka together as father and son."

Minoru felt that the weight of the world had been lifted from his shoulders, for, during those years when he had carried the secret in his heart, he had dreaded the time when he would be forced to share it. Now that it was done, a glad refrain set up in his mind, *I was born of love, I was born of love.* When he finally went up to his bed, the bright streaks of dawn were shooting high through the gray sky.

David McLean made no move to go to bed. How could he hope for sleep until the things revealed to him that night were somehow absorbed and understood? He went into his den and waited until the two stories could blend into an unbelievable whole. Events of his life began to pass in review before him in rapid succession. Had he not then been assured of God's hand to guide him, he knew that he would have the feeling of a fly which had crawled onto a fly-paper. Aloud he heard himself saying, "Lord, what a mess I have made of things. What a mess! All because I was sure that I could handle my life in my own strength and in my own wisdom. From here out, please take over for me."

Like an acorn, the grandfather compared Minoru's love for him, "dropped into my cracked heart."

David felt a sudden deep compassion for this broken-hearted father of Michiko whom he never saw. He also felt a kinship, for again Minoru's love had dropped *like an acorn into his own heart* when it had been shattered by tragedy.

25

As THE STEADY MARCH of Time brought June closer, letters between Seattle and Cleveland flew with regularity. Matsuko became a graduate at nursing school, before Minoru reached the last trying days of his American studies. He was not able to get out to the McLean home, but there was a nightly talk with his new-found father over the telephone. From all accounts things were going well out there. The doctor was working to clear his home desk so that all would be in readiness for his return to the Center on August first.

Minoru kept him informed of the wedding plans, and joyfully reported that he was to have one week in which to get ready for his trip to Seattle. It was planned that David McLean, the best man, would arrive in Seattle the afternoon of the day before the wedding.

One day, David called Minoru, high excitement in his voice,

"I've been thinking, son, what I might give you for your 'graduation' present. What are you planning to do with the week you have managed after work is over at the Center?"

"I have no set plans. There will be packing to do, getting some clothes, and rest I hope. Why?"

"You don't need a trousseau, Minoru, and your things are to be shipped to your boat in New York aren't they?"

"Yes, I am going to take very little with me to Seattle."

"Jake can help you with that as soon as you can get things together. Now listen, my boy, I have plans which include you for that week. Would it be possible for you to join me, with Jake at the wheel to drive us, for a short run into Canada with a few days around Banff? This can be a rest period for us both." The doctor sounded almost jovial.

"Let me come to the house for dinner with you tonight, and we can discuss this," Minoru said.

"Fine idea. I'll send Jake for you around six. If I can talk to you, I know that I can 'twist your arm.' Do you know that expression?" David McLean joked.

"No, I'm afraid that I don't. Remember to explain it to me."

When David McLean turned from the telephone to tell Mrs. Hayes that Dr. Tada would join him for dinner, she noticed that he was as happy as a boy.

"Fine, Doctor. It will be good to have that young man about again. I've missed him; I believe you have too."

Before they had time to realize how the days were whipping by, they were in the car and on their way to Canada. The day they started was one "to put an itch in the foot," David McLean told his son. Then there had followed an explanation of the term's meaning. Always when such a saying from the past was brought up, there was generally one from the Japanese language to match it. Leaving the driving to Jake, they played a sort of game with these ancient sayings. The one which struck David's fancy was the Japanese expression for waiting anxiously to see one. Translated into English it means, "waiting with out-stretched neck."

"That's priceless, Minoru. It calls forth such a picture in one's mind." Saying this the dignified surgeon stretched his neck from his collar, illustrating his mental picture.

"Since coming to America, I have had many Japanese expressions suddenly come to life in English translations. For instance: our good-by — sayonara — it means 'since it must be so!' "

"I think that's beautiful. That is what it is, we don't like it, but it has to be, so we must accept good-bys. Our good-by comes from the old English expression — 'God be with ye'. Did you know that?"

"Never thought about it."

"The Spanish, French and English all come from the same expression, which is natural for the western nations who believe in God."

Jake, hearing the two doctors chatting as they rode along, wondered how two men from different parts of the world could find so much to say to one another. He felt that this was going to be a happy trip for his employer. *That Jap doctor has a lot on the ball. He's nearly pulled Doc McLean back to what he was before his daughter's death.*

On the memorable trip, Minoru realized how much more of a sportsman his father was than he. In the lovely Canadian Rockies' setting Minoru tasted his first experiences of fishing, and golfing on the unbelievably beautiful links. Only in swimming did Minoru find himself an equal to his father. The greatest pleasure of all was the chance to know David McLean more intimately. Watching him closely during these carefree days, Minoru realized that Dr. McLean was a changed man from the shadow he had become after Betsy's tragedy.

It was close timing, but Minoru managed, after his return, to get his packing and shipping done, the things on their way to the boat in New York, and was still able to catch his scheduled flight to Seattle which allowed him two full days before the wedding.

Though he had been in the Hara home only once before this, he knew now that he was no longer a visitor but one of the family. It was his first experience of belonging to a family in the role of a son. Immediately he was swept into the wedding stir with certain responsibilities placed upon him. He waited a bit impatiently for his best man to show up the day before the wedding.

At the hour for the wedding, waiting in the ante room of the church for their signal, the groom and the best man, standing shoulder to shoulder cast admiring glances one toward the other. David M. McLean's heart swelled with pride in his son's solid good looks. *Better still is the person who lives in that beautiful body,* David thought.

Just as their signal was given for them to take their places before the altar, to wait the coming of the bride, David whispered,

"Minoru, have you told Matsuko that by virtue of becoming your bride, she automatically becomes my daughter?"

"No. I didn't want her family to have to absorb so much at such a time. I decided that the story of us can wait until we are on the ocean. It is so involved, it may take the four days of crossing to get it told." They were smiling when they took their places.

While they waited in the tense interval before the bride appeared, and started down the aisle to meet her groom, Dr. McLean let his eyes stray over the guests assembled in the church. They were mostly Japanese. He could hear his father's words, written to him so long ago in Japan, like wisps of fog drifting across the moon, "Project yourself into the future, would you want your mixed-blood children to grow up here? Would you be proud to show them to your family and friends? Would they not even be strange to you? Maybe it would be an injustice to confuse their world for them even before they arrive in it."

A turmoil of emotions surged through his being. *Who could ever be ashamed of a boy like Minoru?* The question shouted in his mind for an answer. For just a moment he brushed his hand across his eyes, then opened them to realize that the bride and her father were standing before the altar and the ceremony was in full swing without his cooperation. Something was still arguing within him.

His thoughts went back to Betsy and her selfish, headstrong ways. He felt his knees begin to grow weak, and, for a minute he felt the panic of the operating room that awful morning when he had failed. The minister's voice was saying at the moment, "May the Lord bless you and keep you. . . ."

"Bless me too, Lord. I need You at this minute. Keep those waves of doubt from overcoming me," David McLean prayed in his heart.

The ceremony was over and David found himself able to follow the bride and groom up the aisle, with the maid-of-honor beside him.

Going home on the plane that night, Dr. McLean pondered the uncertain turns of life. He also gave thanks for the assurance that the Holy Spirit was beside him in his moment of weakness in the church. He had actually felt the strength surge back into his being. He would not doubt again.

No man is wise enough to walk life's way alone. Why doesn't someone go about trumpeting this truth to both young and old?

While David McLean winged his way home, the bride and groom were flying in an opposite direction to Vancouver, a matter of minutes away.

The love which Minoru and Matsuko had to offer each other was new, clean and altogether honest. It was love given in confidence reaching heights which neither of them had dreamed possible. Minoru kept remembering the line from Psalm 19 — "Rejoicing as a strong man to run a race" — a bridegroom coming out of his chamber — ready for a race. Matsuko had been sent to him to make his life complete, and he was ready now for the race which would be his to run.

He would be glad and rejoice to run it once he was back in his country well trained for the work ahead.

They had but a few days in the great Canadian city before they were back in Seattle helping to get their things off by boat across the Pacific to meet them in Japan. Their plans allowed for but two days in New York before boarding the Queen Mary for their real honeymoon and the long way back to the East.

"I don't feel that we need to get a map of New York," Minoru said, once they were settled in a hotel room. "Anything we see here will be new and strange to us, so let's wander."

Hand in hand they did just that, feeling neither strange nor lonely. They were together and all places were home to them.

Once aboard the great ship, they were overwhelmed by the enormous size of it. "Don't you dare get away from me," Minoru warned his bride. "I'd never know where to look for you on this monster."

"Before she sails, let's do some scouting; locate our cabin, then, if we get separated, we can always get back to the cabin and wait for the other to show up. We may not have needed a map in New York, but I definitely need one on this thing."

Systematically they charted their directions: cabin, dining salon, reading room and deck. They were like children in a strange hotel. When the great liner was tugged out to open sea they were in their deck chairs under the bright noon sky, watching the jagged skyline of the city fade into a mauve shadow on the horizon.

When Minoru noticed that Matsuko grew pensive at the thought of letting her country recede and disappear from sight, he took her hand, drew her close to whisper, "Wherever we are together, darling, there it will be home." Matsuko smiled and turned to face him so that he would know that no sacrifice on her part was too much for the happiness which was hers as his wife.

After the excitement of sailing was over, they went to their cabin to settle in for the short trip across the Atlantic. There, on their bed, was a stack of letters. Hurriedly they shuffled through them, seeing that most of them were from Seattle friends who knew how to reach them on the boat. An airmail special was among them from Dr. David M. McLean.

As Minoru tore into the envelope a pink slip escaped and dropped to the floor. Hurriedly retrieving it he noted that it was a check for seventy thousand dollars. He began reading the note aloud:

> My Dears: I almost wish that I were sailing with you this afternoon as you start on your way to Japan. Maybe you'd as soon that I not be along on *this* trip; maybe some day we may have one together. I'm already lonely for you but I'll get used to having you away, but, let's stay close by letter. The pink slip is my gift toward the first unit of the hospital in Takarazuka. Would you, as a favor to me, call it The Takahashi Memorial Hospital in memory of your Mother, Son?

Here Minoru's voice broke; he could not finish the letter.

"Minoru, what is it? What does he mean?" Matsuko asked.

"Darling, now that we are on the way, I have an interesting story to tell you but always it must be our secret. Not even your family must know."

Instead of unpacking, as they had planned to do, they sat side by side upon the bed while Minoru told his story.

"Remember the night at the dinner table in the McLean home, when you seemed to sense a similarity betwen the two of us? Darling, you were right! At that time Dr. McLean knew nothing about it but I had known for years."

Minoru sketched the story for her from the beginning as she sat holding his hand, her eyes wide with unbelief. When he had finished, she sat still turning the amazing story over and over in her mind, asking a question here and there. Minoru held the check in his hands, really not believing what was written there.

Seeing the unfinished letter, Matsuko picked it up to finish reading it aloud.

> Had my first day back at the Center on August first. It's good to be back in harness again. From here out, I'm on firm ground, thanks to you, Dr. Tada.

> Take good care of each other. God's blessings on you both. I shall await to see you again "with out-stretched neck."

> My love to each of you, my children,
> Dad.

"Well!" Matsuko ejaculated, "Isn't it something? I thought I had married a Japanese but it seems that I've married a Scotsman instead."

"Exactly, and that's the reason Scotland is high on our list this trip. Once there, know what I think I shall do? I'll get myself a bit of tartan — McLean plaid, you know. If that doesn't give me enough of my country's flavor, I'll get a bagpipe and learn to play it!"